I0640986

Alexander Shiras

Life and Letters of Rev. James May

Alexander Shiras

Life and Letters of Rev. James May

ISBN/EAN: 9783337137632

Printed in Europe, USA, Canada, Australia, Japan

Cover: Foto ©Raphael Reischuk / pixelio.de

More available books at **www.hansebooks.com**

James May D. D.

LIFE AND LETTERS

OF

REV. JAMES MAY, D.D.,

BY

REV. ALEXANDER SHIRAS, A.M.

" When one that holds communion with the skies
  Has filled his urn where heaven's sweet fountains rise,
  And once more mingles with us meaner things,
  'Tis e'en as if an angel shook his wings.
  Celestial fragrance fills the circuit wide,
  And shows us whence his treasures are supplied."

PHILADELPHIA:
PROTESTANT EPISCOPAL BOOK SOCIETY.
1224 CHESTNUT STREET.

TO

THE STUDENTS WHOM HE TAUGHT,

AND IN WHOM

IT IS HOPED THAT HE MAY LIVE AGAIN,

THIS MEMOIR OF DR. MAY

IS AFFECTIONATELY DEDICATED.

O ALMIGHTY GOD, who hast knit together thine elect in one communion and fellowship, in the mystical body of Thy Son, Christ, our Lord; grant us grace so to follow Thy blessed saints in all virtuous and godly living, that we may come to those unspeakable joys, which Thou hast prepared for those who unfeignedly love Thee; through Jesus Christ, Our Lord.   AMEN.

CONTENTS.

CHAPTER I.

CHAPTER II.

CHAPTER III.

CHAPTER IV.

CHAPTER V.

CHAPTER VI.

APPENDIX.

LIFE AND LETTERS

OF

JAMES MAY, D.D.

CHAPTER I.

EARLY LIFE.

THE virtues of Christians are the riches of the Church. A faithful record of them brings new glory to the Gospel. And the accumulation of such records becomes a history of grace.

When, therefore, a Christian has been moulded by the Spirit to specially near likeness to his heavenly Lord, it seems a duty to photograph, for preservation, the specimen of living Christianity thus given.

Hence this brief memoir of the Rev. James May, D.D. Friends intimately acquainted with the holy beauty of his life, have thought that there was something in it which they could not willingly let die. In hope of blessing to his students and parishioners, perhaps to some besides, that may peruse it, they give a faint sketch of him to the world.

He came, as is usually the case with Christians, of reputable and religious parentage; for though God can gather jewels where He will, He generally takes

2

for the crown of the Redeemer those polished for his purpose in the households of Christ's people.

His mother, a member of the Potts family, of Pottstown, Pennsylvania, was a communicant in the Protestant Episcopal Church, and an intelligent and faithful Christian. His father was an ironmaster of Coventry, in Chester County, Pennsylvania,—a man of large business and lofty character,—so noted in his neighborhood for calm thought and pure integrity, that he was commonly called on to be settler of estates, executor of wills, guardian of orphans, and arbiter in all disputes. He had prospered in his business, both as farmer and as furnaceman, and built himself, in the pleasant valley of French Creek, one of the tributaries of the Schuylkill, a mansion that was almost noble for those days. A meadow sloped from it to the level of the stream, and beyond stretched a fair prospect of fields and farm-houses, garden-grounds and woods, filling the valley, and reaching back into the hills. Here young May first saw the light (October 1st, 1805), and here, beneath the care of judicious and kind parents, whose influence did much to mould his character, he spent most happily the first years of his life. So happy was he in those years, indeed, that he always reverted to them with peculiarly fond memories, and seemed to feel that they had had in them some tastes of Paradise.

They were destined, however, to a painful termination. When James was just entering his eighth year, his father one day undertook to break a strong young horse, and had apparently partially succeeded; but suddenly the animal began to rear and plunge, and, the reins breaking, Mr. May was thrown violently on a stony road. His head struck on a stone, and he was so much injured, that he never woke again to consciousness. He died November 18th, 1812.

This was a fearful darkening of the sky, which previously had been hardly flecked with any clouds. And the shadow thus thrown over the bright life of the household, left its sad traces long behind it. The sunshine never was as clear again, around the home, as it had been before this sorrow. The large business in which Mr. May had been engaged, was either injured by the war with England, which was at that time just thoroughly commenced, or else fell into hands less competent than his to manage it, and ere long was a wreck, of which the farm and home were almost the only fragments.

"Nantes in gurgite vasto."

Sorrow and widowhood told, too, upon the health of Mrs. May. Without the strong hand of her husband to assist her, the care of farm and family together became more weighty than she could endure. The seeds of painful and even torturing disease were before long sown deeply in her system, and after a few years of bitter suffering, borne with a patient Christian faith, she went to lie beside her husband in the little graveyard on the farm. Her death occurred January 17th, 1820; and thus the home that had been once so full of happiness was left desolate.

Before this, however, she had taken prudent care for the education of her children, in order to their making their own way in the world. They all were put in the way to some profession, by which they might sustain themselves if necessary. James pursued his studies at the village school near by his home, till December, 1816. At that time he was sent to Pottsgrove (now Pottstown), to study Latin with his elder brother Thomas, a young man of fine abilities and spirit, then a student for the ministry. Beneath the skilful training of this brother, who had previously had some experience as a teacher, he made considerable progress in the language, and became an unusually accurate scholar for his years. The next season, his brother, just ordained, was chosen Rector of St. John's Church, Norristown, and St. Thomas's, Whitemarsh, Pennsylvania. James removed with him to Norristown, and entered there the Classical Academy, which held almost a collegiate rank. He remained a student at this institution, according to a record made in his own hand, till some time in the year 1821, adding Greek and Mathematics to the studies he had previously been engaged upon. Intensely devoted to these studies, and fired with ambition to excel, a friend that knew him at this time, says it was difficult to detach him from his books and induce him to go forth to play. Perhaps, too, the weight of the sorrows he was passing through, was beginning, even thus early, to depress his spirits, and indispose him for mere frolic sports. For while he was still at the Academy in Norristown, two of the greatest trials of his life fell on him. His brother Thomas, with whom he had been making his abode, had been asked to preach in St. Paul's Church, Philadelphia, and, while there, was called in to see a lady suffering with yellow fever. He took from her the terrible infection of the malady, and died in the full flush of his youthful talents and success, and in the third year of his ministry, September 20th, 1819. And then, early in the next year, came the death of his beloved mother, with the consequent upbreaking of his home. God was fitting him by trial for the tender sympathies of later years. He was darkening the world for him, that he might induce him to seek light from Heaven.

What fruit of *Christian* feeling grew out of these deep griefs, we have no means of thoroughly determining. A record which he kept of the incidents and feelings of those days, has unfortunately been lost, and he was constitutionally too reserved, to let his emotions on such subjects develope themselves before men's eyes, unless they absolutely got the mastery of his firm nerves. It is, however, hardly likely that one so religiously educated as himself, could, twice within four months, part from the dearest Christian relations at the grave-side, without experiencing some drawings of the spirit towards Christ and his kind sympathy—towards Heaven and its peaceful rest. A stream of more than earthly feeling often flows from even rocky hearts, when struck thus with the rod of trial. And James May's heart was not a rocky one. It was as full of fine affections and tender sensibilities as human heart well could be,—moved to intense emotion by even such apparently slight things as a bright scene in a landscape, a soft strain of pensive music, or an affectionately warm greeting from a friend. And such a nature must have felt the need of Christian hope and consolation, when first a mother, then a brother, to both of whom he had been tenderly attached, passed from his already broken family circle to the rest of those that "sleep in Jesus." Still we *know*

2*

nothing in relation to it, except that about this time there was a special seriousness of deportment, and a dwelling in some measure upon spiritual themes. His compositions took the cast almost of sermons, and one of them was so deeply religious in its spirit as to awaken much hope respecting him, amongst his friends. The seed of early Christian nurture was probably beginning, even then, its germination, though the full fruit of a spiritual change was not developed till a later day.

The access of affliction did not diminish in the least his steady purpose to pursue the course of study he had entered on. But, to change somewhat the scenery of life, while still advancing towards the literary culture he desired, we find him the next year, 1821, removed to the house of a half-sister, Mrs. Stevens, the wife of a then ex-governor of Maryland. Their place was in the neighborhood of Easton, Talbot County, on what is termed "the Eastern Shore" of Maryland, *i. e.*, the fertile level region lying between the Chesapeake and the Atlantic Ocean.

There was an excellent school here, under the charge of the Rev. Dr. Alexander Campbell, spoken of as "an eminent Presbyterian divine." In this, our youthful aspirant for education prosecuted still the studies that he had been busy with at Norristown, a son of Governor Stevens, to whom he seems to have been much attached, giving him the encouragement and stimulus of his companionship. Within a year they were so far advanced as to enter together, October, 1822, Stevens the junior, May the senior class, of Jefferson College, Cannonsburg, Pennsylvania. James was at this time only seventeen years of age ; and his ability to enter, at that period, the highest class of a well-conducted college, while somewhat due to the native vigor of his mind, gives ample evidence of his fidelity in study. Through those five years of narrowing circumstances and depressing griefs, he had, with patient and painstaking diligence, laid deeply the foundations of a thorough scholarship, and of the usefulness which it materially promotes. The child was father of the man.

CHAPTER II.

THE college which our youthful student entered had probably been recommended to him by Dr. Campbell. It was an outgrowth from the Scottish Presbyterianism of Western Pennsylvania, and was pervaded by a healthy Christian influence. It had yet hardly passed its infancy,* and had both the advantages and disadvantages of youth. The number of its students still was small, and its endowment scanty. But there was a fresh and vigorous life about it. It was situated in a charming region. The standard of scholarship that it maintained was good. Its President, Dr. Matthew Brown, was admirably fitted for his post; and, to young May, it was no slight recommendation that it was within his native State; for while he was a cordially true patriot, and took the whole Union warmly to his heart, he naturally looked with an especial love on the portion of it in which he had been born and nurtured.

Of course, his entrance on the senior class made necessary only one year's residence at Jefferson. It might have been supposed that this would be too short a time for much impression to be made either by him or upon him. Yet both were done.

He made a good impression upon others. His intellec-

---

* Chartered 1802.

tual ability and patient industry secured him quickly
a high standing in his class. His modest amiability
and obedience to law gained him the good-will of
the Professors. Before the year had ended, he became "a great favorite" with the President; and,
at its close, he shared, with general approval, the
highest honors of the college with a young gentleman who afterwards succeeded Dr. Brown in the
presidency of the institution.

And the best of all impressions was made upon himself,
for he passed here through a decided spiritual change.
His college became to him the place of introduction
to a new and better birth,—birth into a higher life
and a more honorable citizenship. God's chasten-
ings began to yield in him at length the peaceable
fruit of righteousness. They had taught him already
the uncertainty of earthly good, and the desirable-
ness of imperishable treasures. And now that he
was brought into a place where novel Christian influences were around him, and pressing continually
on his notice, he heard the voice of the Divine
awakener within his conscience as he never had before. The death of a beloved sister, about five
months after he had entered college, was blessed
as a means of deepening the feelings which were
already working in his bosom; and realizing finally
his lost condition as a sinner, he began, June, 1823,
to cry out, not in vain, for the creation in him of a
new heart and a right spirit; for though he had
been outwardly blameless to man's view, he now
saw that his inward spirit was all wrong, and that
he needed, not only pardon for his sins, but also
thorough renewal of his nature. It was the voice
of *Law*, however, rather than of *Gospel*, that had

roused him; and he awoke to the darkness of terrible conviction, with yet but little light upon it from the Cross. Oppressed with guilty feeling, he groped on in this darkness for a considerable time, and only through distressing alternations of faint hope and torturing fear emerged at last into the comfortable trust that his transgressions were forgiven and his sins covered.

The change was real; but he did not believe afterwards that it was then complete. It satisfied his friends, but did not satisfy himself. He thought—with good reason, as it eventually proved—that there was something richer in religion than he thus had reached; and it was not till more than a year afterwards, when he had returned from college to his friends in Maryland, that the Holy Spirit cleared thoroughly away for him all difficulties, showing him how, through Christ's obedience unto death for us, the means of perfect salvation is provided, and how, through simple faith in this obedience, as answering for us all the claims of law, the precious benefit and joy of the salvation are attained. Then, taking Christ entirely to his heart as the one only perfect Saviour, he came at length to rapturous enjoyment of the glorious redemption of the Gospel.

God often leads men thus past Sinai to Calvary—subjects them to his government by the brandished rod of Law, and then wins them to his bosom by the opened mercy of the Gospel,—induces first a yielding of the will to him as God, and then a yielding of the heart to Christ as Saviour.

Some think that such a "law-work" is unnecessary. It may not be *essential*. But it forms Christians of decided type. To those who go thus through deep darkness to the Cross, "truly the light is sweet, and a pleasant thing it is for the eyes to behold the sun." A long and terrifying consciousness of sin makes Christ, as Redeemer from it, richly precious; and the soul that has been shaken and agitated with alarms, rests sweetly, and generally steadfastly, in the glorious salvation that secures it peace from them.

It was so in this case. Young May "rejoiced that he was made acquainted with this way of mercy." He wondered that he had not seen before this method of salvation, in which wisdom and simplicity are so strikingly combined. He saw "a beauty" that he "never previously had found" in "righteousness by faith." And *Christ* became to him inestimably dear. "He is to me," says his record of this change, "the shadow of a great rock in a weary land," "the Rock of Ages," "my all in all."

One of the first issues of his spiritual change at college, was a disposition to connect himself immediately with Christ's openly declared disciples. And here came in a demonstration of Christian generosity and delicacy on the part of Dr. Brown, the President, which it would be pleasant to find oftener exhibited. Our new-converted student, with his nephew, who was borne to Jesus on the same wave of religious feeling with himself, called on the President, to consult him as to union with the Presbyterian Church, in which their awakening had taken place. He knew, however, that they had been trained Episcopalians, and, kindly declining to take advantage of their youthful impulse, advised waiting, sober thought, and consultation with their friends at home. With May, this was enough. His

calmly thoughtful mind required only such a touch,
to readjust the wavering balance of his feelings, and
give Church principles an opportunity to operate
again.   He waited ; saw, upon consideration, that
God's awakening of him among Presbyterians did
not bind him necessarily to them; became a member of the Church in which he had been educated;
and though always large-hearted and liberal in his
spirit, never afterwards was shaken from his steadfastness of love for it.   The more ardent Southern
blood of Stevens was not, however, to be calmed.
He pressed his application for admission to the
Presbyterian Church; was eventually welcomed to
it; became finally a minister; and in West Chester,
Pennsylvania, gathered a large and influential congregation, in which he labored, with great acceptance, till his death.

There is little to record respecting Mr. May's
remaining college life.   Pervaded now by the influences of religion, it quietly progressed to a suc-
cessful close.   On the 25th of September, 1823, he
received, with high distinction, the degree of Bache-
lor of Arts, and went forth to make what mark he
might upon the world.

His first intention, influenced by some remaining
wish for earthly wealth and honor, was to study
law.   With this in view, he returned to the house of
Governor Stevens, gathered his law-books around
him, and prosecuted vigorously his studies in that
line for several months.   But deepening religious
feeling would not let him rest in this seeking of
great things for himself. He began to see that there
was something higher to be thought about than personal advancement; something nobler to be lived

for than a comfortable position. in the world,—that Jesus and the Church had claims which must be met, and only could be fully met, in his case, by his entering the Gospel ministry. A change of aim was not, however, made immediately. Self and the world had still some hold upon his heart. He had not come to see yet the full glory of the Saviour, or to realize, from such a sight, the blessedness of a self-denying life, hidden in Christ with God. Visions of great things to be gained by legal study were painfully contrasted, in his view, with ministerial poverty and ministerial exclusion from all lofty place. And it is not wonderful that there occurred, in consequence, a struggle between conscience and ambition—between the feeling that he ought to give himself to Jesus in the ministry, and the desire which still dwelt in him to gain wealth and fame. Nature always combats grace in the beginning: well, if it does not do so to the end. In this case the struggle was a sharp, but not a long one. Christianity and conscience triumphed; and with the feeling that necessity was laid upon him, and that woe was unto him if he preached not the Gospel, he bowed his will to what he thought to be the will of God, gave up his once strong hope of greatness in the world, and resolved, God helping him, to become a minister of Christ.

Such victories of grace bring usually results of comfort. This did, with Mr. May. From a state of distressing inward conflict, which he subsequently spoke of as " the most unhappy period of his life," he passed to an experience of spiritual joy which was like Elim after Marah. He had gone from Maryland to Pennsylvania, to gather books for the study of theology and visit friends residing near his child-hood's home. While there, "one Sunday, after reading the experiences of some true Christians," he retired, for meditation, to a neighboring hill, and " suddenly felt all his powers quickened in devotion." " I beheld God," says he, " by the eye of faith, as a reconciled Father. I beheld an inexpressible love-liness in the character of my Redeemer, and oh! I thought, how could I offend so kind a Saviour! I enjoyed great freedom in prayer, and besought my Redeemer, in consideration of the weakness of my nature and the inefficiency of my resolutions, to grant me grace to enable me to live more near to him, and more devoted to his service. I truly felt joy and peace in believing. At no former period had I enjoyed such a sweetness in religion."

With this sweetness still upon his spiritual taste, he prosecuted for some months his studies in theo-logy, partly while yet with friends in Pennsylvania, partly afterwards at Governor Stevens's, in Mary-land. In October, 1825, he entered the Theological Seminary at Alexandria, D. C., and was found, upon examination, so well grounded, that he was admitted to the Middle Class.

The Seminary thus selected as his school of train-ing for the ministry had been established but three years before, under the auspices of the honored Bishops of Virginia, the Rt. Rev. R. C. Moore, D.D., and his subsequent assistant, the Rt. Rev. William Meade, D.D. It was especially designed to furnish ministers for the Southern portion of the Church, and its aim was to train these not only to a pure and evangelical theology, but also to an elevated Chris-tian character. There were yet only two resident

professors, the Rev. Ruel Keith, D.D., and the Rev.
E. R. Lippitt; the latter of very respectable attain-
ments in Church history; the former eminent alike
for holy spirituality, theological acquirements, and
peculiar aptitude to teach.

Mr. May entered this afterwards celebrated school
in thorough sympathy with its great objects, writing,
as he began his seminary course, "I have come
here to make preparation for the work of preaching
the everlasting Gospel. I trust God has called me
to labor in his cause; and if so, I may rest assured
of his blessing on my preparatory studies. My acquirements are comparatively very limited, and I
have need for great diligence and close application.
Besides human wisdom, I need deep experience in
religion, and a heartfelt acquaintance with the
truths of the Gospel." "I desire constantly to bear
in mind the high vocation wherewith I am called.
And since there is in me no good thing, and no sufficiency to do anything of myself, I desire that all
my sufficiency may be of God through Christ."

And as he thus begun, he seems to have continued, making Luther's maxim essentially his own,
Bene orasse est bene studuisse, and laboring to insti-
tute a holy union of learning and devotion, knowledge and heavenly grace. He gave himself at once
devotedly to study, allowing little time for recrea-
tion, and almost none for those enjoyments of society
which often form the snare of student-life. And as
devotedly did he consecrate himself to effort for
steady advancement in the graces of the Gospel,
aware that learning will not make a minister, unless
associated and interpenetrated with true holiness;
that one must be in sympathy with sacred truth, in

order to a thoroughly effective presentation of it; and must be purely and heartily Christ's follower, in order to win others to his Lord.

A record of the experiences of his Seminary year, shows earnest cultivation of a Christian spirit. Sometimes there are the traces of a conflict amounting almost to an agony, as, laboring to subjugate some special evil in himself, he cries out for divine assistance: "Oh God! have mercy! Leave me not to my own heart! Grant me grace to resist temptation! Deliver me from the dominion of all sin!" And sometimes there are evidences of a clear self-conquest, through the grace which he has thus implored; as when, the old ambition vanishing, he writes, "Dear Saviour, help me to thank thee that thou hast mercifully denied me the splendors of this world! I feel ashamed that I should ever have indulged a wish for the distinctions of it, when thou, who holdest the sceptre of eternal power, didst live despised on earth."

Upon the whole, the progress made upon this field of inward strife appears to have been quite fair for a youthful soldier of the Cross. For though there are no boasts of splendid victories, no vauntings of great spiritual success, we plainly see upon the pages of the journal a deepening humility and growing faith. Sin evidently came to be more dreaded and detested; Christ, to be more trusted in, more honored, and more loved.

Study and silent conflicts with himself were not, however, his sole occupations at the Seminary. The grace that was growing in the student's heart bore fruit of exertion for the Saviour in his life. Besides steady engagement, twice every Lord's day, in the

Sunday-school of Christ Church, Alexandria, we find frequent notices of visits to the prison, to tell those confined there (mostly slaves) of the Redeemer who has preached "deliverance to the captive;" visits to houses of the suffering poor, to administer to them in their afflictions the consolations of the Gospel; and visits to the beds of the aged and the sick, to commune with them in the sacred ordinances of religion, or talk with them of the house not made with hands, eternal in the heavens. And when, about the middle of the spring in the next year, he found it necessary to remove to Philadelphia, to study more immediately under the direction of the ecclesiastical authorities in Pennsylvania, he had grown from a diffident, shy, shrinking student, into a well-experienced Christian, and a workman needing not to be ashamed.

In Philadelphia, where he resumed his studies, after a vacation of about a month, he came, with the consent of Bishop White, under the guidance of the Rev. George Boyd,* Rector of St. John's Church, in the Northern Liberties, a minister of considerable learning, and a very faithful preacher of the Truth. Mr. Boyd was occasionally sent by the Missionary Association of the Diocese on preaching tours through the northern counties of the State, and, knowing thus the wants of the infant churches of that region, was qualified to train his student up for useful missionary labor. The profiting of Mr. May from his instructions in this line eventually appeared to all.

His special object in establishing himself with

---

* Subsequently D.D.

Mr. Boyd in Philadelphia was to prepare himself, by earnest diligence in study, for admission to the Diaconate in the latter portion of the fall. This compression within six months of the studies usually occupying nine, was not infrequent in those early days, when ministers were few, and calls for them often urgent. It involves, however, considerable danger; with *careless* students, of going slightly over subjects; with *conscientious* ones, of injury to health from the exhausting application it requires. Mr. May, belonging to this latter class, bent himself down with resolute determination to full and thorough accomplishment of the whole work. And by economy of time, by careful system, by giving up himself to it entirely, almost to the exclusion of everything besides, he did complete his wearing task, though not in six months, in a little under seven. But he paid for his success the almost inevitable price, in weakened health.

He did not, however, so attend to study as to neglect the cultivation of the heart. The journal still kept of his daily progress gives token of less conflict with temptation, it is true, but evidently because grace was getting gradually the victory, and Christ was putting all enemies under his feet. He was growing in acquaintance with the great salvation of the Gospel, and getting nearer to that happy state in which, reposing thoroughly upon Christ's fulness, faith yields itself to no agitating doubts. The Sunday after his settlement in Philadelphia, there is the record, "Attended at St. John's Church, where I partook of the communion. I found God present with me. I felt the preciousness of Christ. Alas! felt, also, the evil of my own heart. Oh! that my

thoughts were all subjected to my Saviour. Of myself I am nothing; Christ is all in all. My darling
theme now is salvation by faith in Christ, through
God's free grace. When my sins cause me to mourn
and weep, here I look for pardon. Oh! I love my
Saviour; he has done so much for his vile and sinful
creature." And again, shortly after, "Salvation by
grace, how precious! My soul, art thou weary?
Christ is 'the shadow of a great rock in a weary
land.' Art thou tossed on the mountain billows?
He is 'the Rock of Ages,' against which the tempest
beats in vain. Art thou thirsty? Christ says, 'He
that is athirst, let him come unto me and drink.'
Art thou hungering? He is 'the living bread that
came down from heaven.' Art thou weak? He is
thy 'strength.' Art thou sinful? He is 'the Lord
our righteousness.' Art thou complaining of sickness? He is 'the balm of Gilead, and the great
Physician.' Art thou wandering? He is 'the way.'
Art thou in darkness? He is 'the bright and morning star;' 'the sun of righteousness.' What more
dost thou want? *Christ is all in all.*'" Still further,
in the autumn, we find the declaration, "There is
nothing so edifying as the company and conversation of Christian friends. The mutual communication of each other's experience, and talking of the
love of Christ, tend to inflame the heart, and quicken
and encourage in religion. *Since I have been in Philadelphia, I have enjoyed Christian society more than at
any former period of my life.* I have found some who
are truly humble and devoted followers of Jesus.
And I love all who love him."

Henceforth, indeed, his journal gives continual
evidence that grace was keeping pace with know-

ledge, and that rich ripening in the spirit of the Gospel accompanied a growing acquaintance with its truths. It is not, therefore, matter for surprise that, with the high approval of the clergy, he should have passed his various examinations; and that, with like approval from the Bishop, his ordination should have been appointed for the Ember season in December. On the 24th of that month, 1826, he writes: "This day is marked with an occurrence of incalculable moment in my history. I was this morning ordained a deacon by the venerable Bishop White, in Christ Church, in this city. And oh! that God my Saviour would cause me to realize the tremendous importance of my calling. I have set my hand to the plough, and God forbid that I should ever look back." "Preached twice; in the afternoon at St. John's, and in the evening at St. Paul's Church. With a determination to preach the plain and simple doctrines of the Cross, I find it difficult to divest myself of a disposition to cull a flower here and there, and make a nosegay." Did ever youthful preacher fail of such temptation? But the aim was right and high,—such as should ever mark a workman in Christ's field. "*I desire to make the grand subject of my preaching salvation by grace, through faith in Christ Jesus. I pray that this may ever occupy a high place in all my thoughts.*" How truly such became the case, how loftily he held up Jesus and Him crucified, and with what loving spirit he continually lingered around the Cross, all subsequent hearers of his preaching can declare.

CHAPTER III.

BEGINNING his ministerial career with a high character for both ability and piety, our youthful deacon had not long to wait for a field in which to labor for his Lord. The Parish of St. Stephen's, Wilkesbarre, Pennsylvania, was at this time without a minister. It was yet comparatively small, and somewhat agitated by divisions. The salary it offered was hardly large enough to enable even an unmarried man to live; and no minister had, up to 1827, been encouraged to remain there long. But it was in a region evidently destined to be populous. The rich coal-fields and splendid scenery of the Valley of Wyoming lay around it. Besides the townspeople, there was a large and growing country population; and for one that was willing patiently to work and wait, it offered an interesting and attractive sphere of action. Dr. Boyd had often preached there, and knew well the place and people. He told the vestry that, if they desired a Rector, "of all the servants of his Master, there was no one whom he could more cordially recommend to them than James May." The vestry accordingly invited him to visit them, with a view to his settlement among them. Bishop White being informed of it, wrote a letter to the people, speaking of Mr. May in unusually laudatory terms, and saying that in the opinion of himself and other

examiners, they "had seldom found equal sufficiency in the necessary studies for admission to the
ministry." The result was his immediate election
to the Rectorship of St. Stephen's, and his settlement there in February, 1827.

When he thus entered on an independent charge,
Mr. May was little over twenty-one. "He went into
his work," says Dr. Stone, "in appearance, as well
as in reality, a mere youth, with fresh complexion
and dark glossy hair, an object of naturally pleasing
interest; and though at first painfully diffident, he
speedily won, and what he won never lost, the hearts
of all his people." If any had supposed that his
youth and inexperience would hinder his early at-
tainment of much influence, they soon found their
mistake. Almost before one could have deemed
it possible, the little divisions in the Parish were
forgotten, and a united, loving, and harmonious
congregation welcomed the ministry of the young
pastor. This was not through the influence of a
commanding eloquence, or the geniality of an especially attractive character, for his abilities had not
reached yet their full development, and youthful
diffidence still threw a shade of distance and reserve
over his address. But it was, under God, through a
wisely quiet prudence, which utterly ignored the existence of divisions, and cautiously abstained from
word or act that might fan any old ember of excitement into flame. It was through a serene and pious
dwelling in such an elevated Christian atmosphere,
as worldly influences could hardly venture to invade.
It was through instant, full engagement in ardent
labors for the advancement of Christ's cause, giving
the people something better to attend to than trifling

differences about personal or Church affairs. And it was through such an obvious and open honesty of purpose to know nothing among them but Jesus Christ and Him crucified, as left no room for any doubt that he was a true and faithful servant of the Saviour.

If there was any jarring element that survived the first few weeks of intercourse, it was one that quickly vanished, like the rest. This was a disposition on the part of one or two to awaken doctrinal debates. There had been a suspicion (not uncommon in those days respecting every earnest preacher), that the new minister might be a Calvinist. Quick ears watched, therefore, every pulpit utterance. But when they heard nothing about reprobation or election, and found that the free offer of acceptance in Christ Jesus had no restriction but the one of wilful unbelief, debate had no ground left on which to plant its batteries, and suspicion was soon fairly in retreat. The very ones that seemed most prepared to cavil, became finally the warmest friends of Mr. May.

Thus, prudence, goodness, and a pure adherence to God's word, will ever win their way at last to men's regard. And thus God gave the youthful shepherd, before long, the cordial confidence, not only of the flock he guided, but also of the whole community in which he moved. An excellent old gentleman, not a member of his congregation, used sometimes, quietly, to say to friends, that he had his fears respecting Mr. May, for there was a woe to them of whom " all men " should speak well.

Of course, with such a minister, the congregation of St. Stephen's grew. Men that had never pre-

viously attended, began to be found within the sanctuary. Loose hangers-on became regular attendants.
A fair proportion of the intelligence, cultivation, and
piety of both Wilkesbarre and its neighborhood, clus-
tered around the man whom all respected and many
were beginning ardently to love. And, ere long,
full audiences, devout, respectful, and heartily engaged, rewarded the efforts of the young pastor in
his church. This, too, although the other Christian
congregations in the place were favored at the same
time with a very able ministry; and although, in
one of them (the Presbyterian), the afterwards celebrated Dr. Murray (Kirwan) was then officiating, in
the first flush of his great powers.

This success, however, was not reached through
personal influence alone. It was assisted, doubtless,
by that reverence for goodness which seems a rem-
nant of man's first estate. But it had other grounds.
Mr. May was a faithful and most earnest preacher
of the Gospel. He never tired of presenting its inestimable truths. He dwelt affectionately and constantly on the provision God had made in Christ for
the redemption of our sinful race. He showed how
freely all the benefits of that redemption were offered
by a gracious Saviour. He pointed to the generous
willingness of God to give the Spirit unto them that
ask him, to enable them to turn from sin and lay hold
on the Redeemer. And he urged his hearers, with
all the tenderness of pleading, tearful love, to go, beneath the guidance of the offered Spirit, to the Saviour, stretch out to him the hands of faith and
prayer, and take what he was ready to bestow on them,
a full salvation. Eager to bring these Gospel mes-
sages to bear more constantly and closely on the

hearts of all his flock, he established numerous weekly services, which, up to this time, had been almost unknown amongst his people. One was held on Monday evening for the young, one on Wednesday evening for the congregation generally, and one on Friday, of a more social and informal character, for the members of the church. To these was added, soon, a Bible class on Saturday.

To most men at that date, such frequent services, in addition to two on the Lord's day, would probably have seemed abundantly enough to meet entirely the responsibilities of their position. But to Mr. May there was no limit of responsibility, save that of the utmost exertion of his strength. And as he saw, beyond his congregation, a considerable rural population, with no churches in its midst, he felt that he must go as far as to these, also, preaching the Gospel of Christ. He instituted, therefore, first one religious service for them, then another, till he had four regular stations in the country, at each of which he officiated twice a fortnight—once on Sunday and once in the week—making thus, with his appointments in Wilkesbarre, four Sunday services and one every week-day. It was too much for a parish clergyman to undertake. No one but an evangelist like Whitefield and the Wesleys, continually travelling, and not bound up to in-door work, can safely tax his strength to such an extent. Mr. May eventually paid dearly for it. But it was beautiful evidence of his devotion to Christ's cause, his love for souls, and his willingness to spend and be spent for their salvation. It did great good, too. It brought multitudes to listen to the Gospel that might never otherwise have heard it. It was the means of leading not a few to Jesus.

And it sowed good seed in many neighborhoods, that is still springing up and bearing fruit unto eternal life.

In a letter, written quite late in his life, he describes the first institution of these country services. It is dated at Philadelphia, July 8, 1861, and says, " I never preach with more spirit than to such an audience of honest, simple-hearted hearers as assemble in your school-house on Sunday nights. Such hearers I was accustomed to speak to in years long gone, some of whom, too, I followed to their graves. My first essays at this kind of preaching were on a barn floor, in the Valley of Wyoming, in a neglected neighborhood, where was neither church nor school-house. Active Sunday-school teachers procured the use of a large barn during summer, and employed the farmer to sweep it out every Saturday afternoon, and place boards on stones or blocks for benches (the normal shape of pews); and there, with the great doors thrown open, we enjoyed shade and cool breezes, without being disturbed by any articulate sounds, or impatient motions of oxen and horses, which were feeding in their stalls on our right hand and on our left."

" After the duties of the Sunday-school in that model room, the religious services and preaching came on. You may imagine how a young deacon would speak in such circumstances. So one did speak every Sunday afternoon, till we advanced to the dignity of a log school-house."

" Would you think it a marvel, if I should say that one of the hearers there was a boy who afterwards rose to the office of Attorney-General of Pennsylvania? It was even so."

The services thus spoken of were all held subsequently in the little school-houses of the several neighborhoods, generally two or three miles from town. They were well attended by a plain, substantial people, mostly the small farmers and laborers around. The prayers were brief; the singing animated; the preaching, simple Gospel truth, set in the sunlight of familiar illustration, and perfectly pure English words. Mr. May never suffered himself to be kept from them, if it was at all possible for him to be there, though sometimes his resolution was severely tasked. On one occasion, a blinding tempest had set in, before the time for service, and snow and sleet were sweeping down the hills, along the road that he must travel to his post. His friends expostulated with him against turning out in such a storm. But he said the rugged country people, accustomed to exposure, would probably be out, and he could not disappoint them. He started, but the dashes of the impetuous wind and sleet soon drove him back into the house. Again he made the effort, and again was driven back. But when there came a little lull, he once more set resolutely forth, and with iron will pressed on against the blasts, to find the people, as he thought he should, gathered for worship, and expecting him. Of course, that settled for him the question about keeping his appointments at all risks; as *his* presence settled for the country people the question of their attendance in all circumstances.

From all this sowing of the Gospel seed, fair harvests were naturally to be looked for. They came in their due time. God did not let his word return unto him void. First gradually and silently, then in full shower, the influences of the Holy Spirit were poured out upon the field so industriously cultivated. And beneath those influences the seed that had been sown sprung up, and bore its fruit. A great improvement in the spirit of the Christian portion of the congregation was the first visible result. Then came the quiet addition of one and another thoroughly converted soul from the world to the communion,—not many, but every one a real accession to its strength. And, finally, after about five years of prayerful labor, there was granted to the patient pastor such an ample spiritual blessing as promised for awhile to bring bodily into the Church almost all the previously unconverted portion of the people. More than seventy persons came in a single day, after a series of religious services, to ask their minister to guide them in the way to an eternal life; and, had he been ambitious of the reputation to be gained by mere numerical additions to his church, he might have swept at once into its communion almost the whole of these inquirers after Christ. But, cautious to an extreme as to admission to church membership, and believing that true strength came from pure character, not lengthened lists, he brought comparatively few of the whole number to the sacraments, and these not until after months of preparation. Of the rest, some were not admitted to communion for a year; others, not until after a still longer time.

The caution thus displayed is mentioned as a fact. How far it should be followed as a pattern, there may be difference of views. Undoubtedly the Church has suffered much from hasty and inconsiderate additions. Undoubtedly, one well-proven subject of

God's grace is worth many dubious ones. But as undoubtedly there must be great indulgence for the first weaknesses of Christian feeling,—a remembrance that the just-awakened are but "babes in Christ,"—and a gentle recollection that there must be "first the blade, then the ear, afterwards the full corn in the ear." Religious feeling, in our fallen nature, is such a tender, delicate exotic, that ordinarily it must be early housed within the Church; and even there the husbandman must have "long patience" in looking for bright blossomings and precious fruits. The ones whom Jesus called to be his special followers were very imperfect Christians at the outset; and it took three years of intercourse with him, and then a large outpouring of the Spirit, to make them all that they required to be. And where the Master leads the way, the minister may safely follow.

Another season brought another wave of seriousness along with it, due in some measure, under God, as was the last, to the kind labors of a "Clerical Association," but still more to the blessing of the Spirit on the faithful pleading of the pastor with his flock. The services of the Association, held for some days in the church, were drawing to a close, with seemingly but slight results, when he arose, and with a melting pathos which instantly affected every heart, implored the unconverted portion of his people not to let slip that golden opportunity for going to their Saviour, and seeking life and peace through him. Ten minutes of the tenderest exhortation followed; and when it ended, there was not apparently a tearless eye nor unaffected spirit in the church. All dropped upon their knees in prayer for blessing; and men that had been quite unused to weep were overflowing with emotion. A considerable subsequent addition to the Church was the result, though, as before, not what it might have been, and would have been, under a caution less extreme than Mr. May's.

And so it went on, till the church in Wilkesbarre, from a feeble missionary station, grew to be what it has ever since continued, the largest, strongest, most effective one of the Protestant Episcopal communion in all that section of the Diocese,—full of a living, working Christianity, and of those fruits of righteousness which are, through Jesus Christ, to the glory and praise of God.

The Pastor of St. Stephen's had not been *alone* in all these pleasant experiences with his flock. On the 8th of January, 1829,—two years after his settlement in Wilkesbarre,—he had wedded ELLEN STUART BOWMAN, daughter of Captain Samuel Bowman, of his parish, and sister of the Rev. Samuel Bowman, afterwards Assistant Bishop of the Diocese of Pennsylvania. No marriage union could well have been happier than this proved. It was one of the matches that seem truly "made in heaven." To supplement the sterling sense and devout piety of Mr. May, Miss Bowman brought personal graces, mental endowments, and a Christian spirit of a very lofty order. She held the doctrines of the Gospel with a clear discrimination, and placed before herself the highest standard of a purely Christian life. How nearly she approached that standard in the clear beauty of her life-long walk, none that were well acquainted with her need be told. She was one of the happy characters whom all unite to praise. "When the eye saw her, then it blessed her; and when the ear heard her, it gave witness to her." She shed life through every company she entered, and joyful sunshine round her husband's home.

In the household, her neatness, taste, domestic order, hospitality, and piety, were conspicuous at once. The study was directly made as comfortable as wifely hands could make it. The family Bible was assigned a place upon a stand designed especially to bear it. The domestic worship was studiously attended to, as the central point of interest; and every effort was industriously used to make the home, for all that entered it, as happy and as holy as an earthly home might be.

In the parish, she aided officially in all associations of the female members of the Church for religious and charitable objects; while in the Sunday-school she taught, with great efficiency, a large and interesting infant class.

Thus bound anew to his people and the place by ties of the sweetest and most pleasing character, it is no wonder that, when calls to other fields were made, Mr. May should have shrunk from the acceptance of them. Entirely happy in his home and in his work; blessed in himself, and made a blessing to his people, he seemed to have no aspirations left for anything on earth beyond what he enjoyed. The invitations to attractive points which reached him, he, therefore, quietly turned over to his Vestry, as the representatives and executive committee of his congregation. And when he was assured by them, as he was repeatedly, of their high estimate of his services among them, with their desire to preserve him for their church, as well as all that portion of the Diocese, such matters immediately

ended with him. He seemed to put them out of
mind entirely. But he certainly could not have put
out of mind the kind expressions of his Vestry on
one of these occasions. " When you first came to
this people, you found them divided and broken,
burdened with debt, and few in number. The
influence of your character and your exertions
have healed these dissensions, have enabled them to
free themselves from their incumbrances, and have
formed them into a respectful body of attentive
hearers. What schisms and difficulties your departure and their choice of a successor may lead to, He
only with whom there is no future can tell, and time
alone make known to us."

At length, however, the dreaded hour of separation came. The long morning sunshine of his residence in Wilkesbarre drew to a close. He had received, October, 1836, a call to the Rectorship of St.
Paul's Church, Philadelphia, then vacant from the
election of the Rev. Samuel A. McCoskry to the
Episcopate of Michigan. He did not incline to the
acceptance of it, and told his Vestry so, to their
great joy. But the pleadings of many ministerial
friends were thrown into the scale of the invitation
to St. Paul's, and notwithstanding the opposing
pleadings of deep-rooted and sincere attachment to
his charge, he at last began to hesitate. His people
grew uneasy, and used every effort to retain him;
but finally they had to yield. A ministerial brother,
by one quick, decisive blow, bore down the wavering balance on the Philadelphia side, telling him,
that pleasant as it might be for him to be cultivating
his little flower garden in the country, he owed it to
his Master to assume the duties of the wider and

much more laborious field to which so many voices called him. That was enough. The thought that for mere personal considerations, he might be evading a clear call of duty to Christ's cause, determined him to go to Philadelphia. So, amidst many tears, he gave his final charge to his beloved flock in Wilkesbarre,* and with a deeper grief than he dared utter, turned from his happy valley home, to work for Jesus amidst city streets, commercial bustle, and the crowd and shock of men.

---

* That final charge is worthy of republication. It is full of the very marrow of the truth as it is in Jesus, and of a tender persuasiveness that is touching in the extreme. After telling the people of the pain with which he parts from them, and the great happiness he has enjoyed amongst them, he counsels the Christians of his church to hold fast the foundation of safety and peace laid for them in Jesus Christ, to study more and more to know Christ, to cultivate the religion of the closet, to be diligent in prayer and study of the Scriptures, to cherish love for one another, and for the members of the other churches round. And then, turning to those not yet connected with Christ's people, he reminds them of his labors for their spiritual benefit, and pleads with them to seek instant pardon and acceptance before God in Christ; to offer themselves to him who claims their all, and in his love find what the riches of a world could not supply. And finally, he says, "I now take leave of all my late parishioners, knowing well, that a more affectionate people I shall find in no place whithersoever I may go. My dearly loved friends, a burden is on my heart while I leave you. I shall have many an affectionate remembrance of you. I commend you to God, who will not forsake you. I pray for his grace to abide with you, for his love to be in your hearts evermore. My heart's desire is, that after having followed Christ our Saviour in his temptations, we may all meet at his table in the kingdom of the Father."

CHAPTER IV.

It was in February, 1837, that, from the mountains covered with their drifted snows, the departing pastor took his last sad look at the town, and church, and school-houses, in which, for ten most happy years, he had labored for his Lord. Before the month closed, he was at his work in Philadelphia with all his wonted earnestness. A goodly number of the members; of the church gave him their warm co-operation there. Ears long accustomed to the sound of the pure Gospel at St. Paul's, perceived the clear ring of its truths in the utterances of their new minister; and hearts that loved the spirit of that Gospel embraced in their affections the beautiful and holy exhibitions of it, apparent in the walk of both himself and Mrs. May. And neither he nor his admirable wife were persons to withhold, from any demonstration of affection, a hearty and sincere return. They learned to love most truly the members of the flock in Philadelphia, and quickly formed, with some of the good people there, close intimacies, that continued throughout life.

Such men, too, as the Rev. Dr. Tyng, John A. Clark, William Suddards, and the like, extended cordially the hand of ministerial welcome, and did all they could to make their new associate feel at home.

Of course these things attached him closely to his church, his people, and the friendly clergy named. But yet, to old familiar friends, it was evident that the transplanted tree was not entirely at its ease in the new soil. Its roots bled secretly. Its foliage drooped. The fresh, pure, vigorous life it had exhibited in its old seat, came very slowly back to it.

The truth was, there were some disadvantages about the change which had been made, that hindered comfortable settlement.

In the first place, Mr. May had not been wholly clear, in his own mind, as to the duty of removal to St. Paul's. He had rather yielded to the judgment of his brethren, than formed a decided conclusion for himself; and in such circumstances, a deeply conscientious man is apt to be disturbed by occasional uprising doubts respecting the propriety of his own action in the case.

Then, too, the Vestry of the church in Wilkesbarre had not entirely given up their hold upon him. Aware of his preferences for a country charge, and thoroughly assured of his attachment to them, they kept their pulpit open for a year and more, in the declared hope of having him return to it. And, kind as the feeling was that led to this, it naturally kept up some unsettled questionings whether there ought to be a continuance or a return. For, strong as were the ties that had been formed in Philadelphia, there were, of course, many drawings of the heart towards the pleasant home, the little missionary stations, and the bright scenery of his first church-love.

Perhaps because of this, there was no dwelling taken, and no real *home* formed in the city. He boarded; and though with pleasant people, and in pleasant nearness to his church, all know how much less deeply the roots of the affections strike about a mere sojourning place, than they do about *a home*.

And, finally, his honest modesty stood in his way. He came, at St. Paul's, in close successorship to two men of much more than usual note; one, the most energetic pastor that either that or any other church could well have had, the Rev. Dr. Tyng; the other, a minister distinguished, in a high degree, for social attractiveness and oratoric grace, the newly elected Bishop of Michigan. In contrast with such men, the new incomer, wont to underestimate himself, hardly felt as if he could command, for his clear,* unadorned presentments of the Gospel, the audience that had been given to the splendid talents of one predecessor, and the pleasingly attractive manners of the other. It was a needless feeling, but it was sincerely entertained, and it discouraged him.

The shadow of these things was thrown across the sunshine of his life in Philadelphia, and sometimes, in consequence, there was a painful gloom. With his calm, conscientious steadfastness, this did not hinder full devotion to his work. But it did long hinder his enjoyment in it. He went at it with a hearty will, and did it with a pure fidelity. No tittle of it was neglected. No portion of the strength God gave for it, was unused. In church, in lecture-room, in prayer-meeting, and in Sunday-school, he was still the clearly faithful preacher of the Gospel, and loving herald of "the Lamb of God that taketh away the sin of the world." He even added to his

---

* "So clear, so shining, and so evident,
    That they might glimmer through a blind man's eye."

arduous pastoral labors, other work, which his predecessors had not done—such as the editorship of the Episcopal Recorder. which he undertook in union with the Rev. Messrs. Clark and Suddards, and the Rev. Dr. Tyng. And what a golden age of editorship that was, the older Episcopalians of Philadelphia well remember. But amidst all labors, the shadow lay along the path for a long period, and he was slow in coming out into the brightness of the old genial home-feeling that he had in Wilkesbarre.

Doubtless to some extent in consequence of this, as well as in consequence of his excessive labors in the Valley, there came, before very long, symptoms of failure in his health. His voice lost something of the clearness of its ring, and other tokens of a painful Laryngitis showed themselves. The disease was battled with for a considerable time, before the energetic laborer would at all consent to yield. But, at last the advice of physicians was emphatic, that there should be a retirement from exhausting pastoral work. A voyage to Europe, and a temporary rest from all public exercise of voice, was recommended, and finally determined on. Leave of absence for a year was voted by the Vestry, in the hope that by the expiration of that time he might return restored. By most men, such a leave would probably have been accepted almost as a right, and all the perquisites of office have been held still, as a thing of course. But with Mr. May the standard of clerical action was a high one. He questioned whether a minister of Christ should draw a salary which he was not earning by his labor. And he did not wish to hold the Church bound to him while he was a wanderer, uncertain as to the restoration of his health, and consequently as to the time of his return to duty. He therefore, before leaving, sent in to the Vestry his resignation of the Rectorship, thus cutting himself off, as far as his own action could effect it, from all claim to salary, and putting it within their power to call, in place of him, whom they might please. The resignation was not handed in by the gentleman to whom it was intrusted, till Mr. May, informed of its retention, wrote back to urge that it should be offered as designed. Then, with a generosity very properly answering to his, the Vestry declined action on it, in the expressed trust that God's good providence would yet restore him to themselves and to the Church.

Of the feeling entertained respecting him at his departure, and of the impression he had made on those associated with him while in Philadelphia, some estimate may be formed from the language of an editorial notice of him, published at this time in the Episcopal Recorder. After giving an account of the failure of his health, and departure for a European voyage, the writer says: "We have no words to express our estimate of the worth of our brother to the Church. We have never yet heard the preacher of the Gospel, whose views of divine truth were more clear, searching, instructive, and powerful. We have never seen the man, whose life was more accordant with the Gospel he proclaimed. He is a mighty and a holy man. When such a one is laid aside from the ministry in the very spring of his maturity, and the Church is deprived of his inestimable labors, it is a trying judgment. We beg our friends, and the friends of the Gospel of Christ, to pray for his recovery,—to beseech the Lord of the harvest that such a laborer, so qualified, so tried, so approved, so competent, may not be taken out of the harvest."

Followed by many such demonstrations of esteem, and attended by Mrs. May and a valued female friend from Philadelphia, Mr. May embarked at New York for Havre, October 24th, 1838. The days of ocean steamships were then just beginning, the first regular passages being made this very season by the Sirius and Great Western. There were none for French ports yet; and the party accordingly took passage in the sailing packet Poland. Five weeks were spent upon the ocean, and the bleak winds of winter began to make themselves perceived, when, on the 1st of December, the voyagers awoke to find themselves within the port and by the quays of Havre. The enthusiasm of the French portion of the passengers at seeing once again their native soil, communicated something of its glow to their transatlantic company, as they landed for their long sojourn amidst foreign sounds and scenes.

A Sabbath rest was taken,* amidst all the Sabbath bustle of the French,—thanks offered for their preservation on the sea, and their future way committed to the Lord. Then, as soon as possible, they were on the road to Paris, admiring the beauty of the Valley of the Seine, and finding in its venerable towns, quaint chateaux, and vine-covered hill-sides, points of inte-

---

* Such was the regular rule with these true Christian travellers, when on land, and with their movements under their control. Never was sacred time invaded by a journey. Nor was it desecrated by mere sight-seeing, either in the Romish Church or other ways; but always devoted to true *worship* in Protestant sanctuaries, or in the privacy of their own rooms.

resting contrast with the new world from which they came.   Two weeks in Paris gave them considerable knowledge of its chief localities, many works of art, and then rapidly increasing Christian privileges. That accomplished, they were off for Italy, fleeing from wintry storms to its bland atmosphere,—from snow-clad landscapes, to its still green and sunny scenes.   At Marseilles, they stopped a moment to renew acquaintance with a French family whom they had known in the Valley of Wyoming; then, launching forth on the steam-packet for the South, were soon again on the blue waters of the sea.   Oppressive sea-sickness induced a landing of our travellers at Leghorn; thence a run up the Valley of the Arno, to see the beauties of Florence and its neighborhood; and then a journey by the road across the hills to Rome.   Naples became the centre of their winter sojourn, excursions being made at intervals to all the classical localities around its splendid bay, and even down into Calabria.   As spring advanced, the line of march was taken up again for Northern Italy, amidst the glorious scenery of which some charming days were passed.   The early summer was devoted wholly to the grandeur of the Alps, and to the lakes and towns of Switzerland; later July to the beauties of the " castled Rhine," and of the border lands of Germany.   In August, the Low Countries were gone over, Paris visited again; and then, with eager steps, England and Scotland, Ireland and Wales, were sought, nine months of sojourn and travel on the Continent having made them hungry for the home-like institutions, the familiar language, and especially the Christian influences of these well-known sister lands.   And great indeed was their enjoyment, not only of the scenery and antiquities of Britain, but also, and still more, of the services and the society of such men as Baptist Noel, T. S. Grimshawe, Edward Bickersteth, Josiah Pratt, and other kindred followers of Christ. To sit beneath the ministry of men that preached the Gospel as these did, or to commune with them in private intercourse about the interests of the Redeemer's cause, was, to these ardent Christian souls, a religious luxury superior to sight-seeing, having tastes in it of "the marriage-supper of the Lamb." They loved the image of the Saviour in his people: they loved a hearty, earnest proclamation of his truth: they loved a Gospel, that, reverently and affectionately, made "him first, him last, him midst and without end." And in the leaders of "the Evangelicals" in England, they found all that they sought in these respects, and were most richly satisfied.

At London, on their return from Ireland in October, the friend that had accompanied them thus far took leave of them, to return to the United States, the advice of experienced English physicians being that Mr. May should spend another winter in South Italy, and probably the whole remaining portion of a second year abroad. After some new conscientious questionings as to what was duty in the case, Mr. May had resolved to follow this advice. Renewing, therefore, to his Vestry the offer of a resignation made to them a year before, he and Mrs. May turned their faces once more toward the Continent, on the 11th of November, 1839.

There was some natural sadness at starting thus again in a direction opposite to that which they had hoped to follow. The memories of home and

friends and country had been re-awakened by the
flag that floated at so many mast-heads in the English ports.   The thought of restoration to their
waiting church and people had been warmly entertained.   And to have to give all up, to leave even
the country which had seemed to them the most like
home of all in Europe, and plunge once more amidst
the foreign tongues and habits from which they re-
coiled, was no slight test of their serenity of trust in
God.   But faith was strong, and triumphed.   They
knew in whom they had believed, and could not
doubt that he was making all things work together
for the good of those that loved and trusted him.
Without a murmur, therefore, though not, possibly,
without a sigh, the arrangements for another year's
sojourn abroad were made, and on the 11th of November, they were on their way again towards
Italy.   The footsteps of their former journey South
were retrodden for the greater portion of the way;
only, this time, the journey *closed* at Rome.   Their
winter-quarters were established on the Pincian Hill
there, and the cold months spent in renewed study
of the language, in re-examination of the antiquities
and works of art, and in the enjoyment of a pleasant
Christian intercourse with friends from America and
England.*   They saw, whenever they could be seen

---

* In a letter to a cousin, under date of January 1st, 1840, Mr.
May gives the following picture of their home life while in
Rome:

"We are in some sense keeping house, *i. e.*, we hire furnished
lodgings, the necessary furniture for the table being included; and
then we buy all our own groceries, and have our bread, butter
and milk sent in.   Our dinners are either sent ready cooked from
a Traiteur's, or we go out and get them, as we please.   A card
being furnished, on which are the names of several hundred dishes,

upon the week-days, the peculiar ceremonies of the Papal Church, getting from all they witnessed of its working, in this its very central seat, such deepening convictions of its superstition and idolatry, as made them stronger Protestants than ever. To test how far the Bible was allowed to circulate where Romanism had all things its own way, inquiry was once made for it at a number of the book stores, but for some time utterly without success. At last, one bookseller said he had it, yes; and handed down a whole shelf-full of books, the Bible, but so overlaid with commentaries, that it was almost impossible to find the text, amidst the mass of cumbersome interpretations. Yet such, as far as could be ascertained, was the only copy of the Holy Scriptures at that time for sale in Rome! The Roman revolution, nine years afterwards, introducing a liberal Republic for a time, afforded opportunities, which Christians were

---

with the price affixed to each, we can make a selection according to our taste, our appetite, our purse, or all together. Our dinners cost from twenty to twenty-five cents each. But to-day being New Year's day, we launched out into one of the most extravagant dinners we have yet ordered in Rome. We prescribed roast turkey, lamb cotelettes, vegetables, cauliflowers, custard, &c. &c., and, when we came to the reckoning, paid a bill of *thirty-two baiocchi and a half* each,—exactly thirty-two and a half cents of our money,—and came home quite filled with our feast.

"You would no doubt laugh if you could come into our parlor in the morning, when we are preparing breakfast. Our Donna (the servant woman of the house) brings in our tea-kettle, and puts it on the fire. Then, while Ellen (Mrs. May) gets her teapot ready, if we are in a hurry, I take the bellows and 'raise the wind.' Our bread, butter, &c., being furnished us regularly from a shop, we soon get all prepared, and sit down as independently as the Pope himself. We are by no means peculiar in our mode of living, but are *in the Italian style.*"

not slow to use, for considerable circulation of the
sacred Word; though, probably, upon the reinstate-
ment of the Papacy, it became as scarce as ever at
the stores again.

Of course, amidst such proofs of misgovernment
and tyranny, the growth of *patriotism* in our travellers kept pace with that of *Protestantism.* They were
true citizens of the United States. Genial and
friendly with the foreigners whom they were thrown
in contact with, and fully appreciative of whatever
might be good, in them, their institutions, or their
social ways, the *amor patriæ* still deepened in their
breast with every month that they remained abroad.
And often, as they caught a glimpse of the ensign
of their country, or saw how, elsewhere, the people
were oppressed, there was a disposition to hurrah
for the Republic, as, of all governments, the best,
the happiest, and the most intelligently free.

Nor was this feeling lessened in the least when,
the next spring after their wintering in Rome, they
made a visit to the Grecian Archipelago, stopped for
awhile at Athens, and then, crossing to Alexandria,
went up the Nile. The beauty of the isles of
Greece, the interest and grandeur of the antiquities
of Egypt, although observed with eager spirit, could
not blind eyes that had been trained here in America to the hard selfishness of the government of
Otho, and the fierce tyranny of Mohammed Ali and
his sons.

The condition of the Coptic Church in Egypt engaged considerable attention, while at Cairo; and a
painful picture of its miserable degradation is given
in the journal kept by Mr. May. The priests, he
learned, were utterly uneducated, taken in general

from the lowest classes of the people, and compelled to serve, whether willing or unwilling, in the office to which they were almost forcibly ordained; the only training of most of them for their work being in mechanical repetition of the services. As might naturally be expected in such circumstances, the standard of religion and morality was low, the people almost wholly untaught in the Gospel, and the prospect of improvement from within the Church extremely faint. The only solid hope of benefit seemed, under God, to be in influences from without, especially in the schools conducted for the Copts by missionaries from the Church of England.

It had been intended, in this journey East, to go from Egypt into Palestine. And it was a grievous disappointment when, after every preparation for the sacred pilgrimage was made, reports of the prevalence of plague in Syria induced, at the last moment, an abandonment of their intention, and a precipitate return to Greece.

Here, time enough was spent to allow considerable examination, not only of the monuments of ancient art, but also of the noble schools at Athens, conducted as a Protestant Episcopal Church Mission by the Rev. J. H. and Mrs. Hill. And so satisfied was Mr. May, from this examination, of the beneficent influence of this Mission on the Greeks, and the general wisdom of the action of its managers, that he remained from that time forward the steadfast advocate of this great work.

A month at the Piræus and in Athens, with views of the mountains about Corinth, of Eleusis, of Salamis, of Eubœa, and of Marathon, sufficiently satisfied the curiosity of the travellers respecting East-

ern Greece.   Then, taking passage in the steamer
for Trieste, a sight was had of the bare mountain
groups of the Morea, of the fine scenery around the
Gulf of Corinth, and of the islands of the Western
Coast, green, rich, and fair, in comparison with the
stern rocks, which, for the most part, form the Cy-
clades.

They entered the harbor of Trieste, rejoicing to
find all around them ships from their own country,
and to see floating freely out upon the breeze the
familiar stars and stripes.

From Trieste to Vienna, from Vienna on to
Prague, from Prague to Dresden, from Dresden to
Berlin, gave them a view of the fairest parts of Aus-
tria, of the scene of the ministry of Huss and Je-
rome in Bohemia, of the magnificent art galleries of
Saxony, and then of the points where Luther and
Melancthon labored and taught for Christ.   To the
work of the Reformers, the heart and mind of the
two united travellers turned with intensest interest.
They had seen, lately, enough of the corruption of
the Roman and Greek Churches to understand,
better than ever previously, from what a depth of
evil these agents of God's goodness had rescued the
German Church.   And when they came upon the
field where the standard-bearers in the work had
lifted up an ensign to the nations, they traced with
eager zest the points of start, the lines of march, and
the chief scenes of conflict in that great fight of
faith.   The studies in which Luther and Melancthon
wrote, the University in which they taught, the pul-
pits from which they had preached the Gospel, the
church door upon which the famous theses had been
nailed, the spot on which the burning of the Papal

bull took place, and other memorials of the great lives which were, almost throughout, one long, brave battle for the truth, were gone over, with devout thanksgiving to him who clothed the warriors with their armor, and gave them glorious victory in the war.

Then, after brief enjoyment in the capital of Prussia, way was made again to England. And here the cream of their whole European trip seems to have been gathered up. They had in Italy, and on the voyage north from Greece, met members of the Christy, Braithwaite, Buxton, and Gurney families. Congeniality of tastes and kindred Christian feeling had drawn them towards each other, and a strong mutual attachment and esteem was the result. And when they came once more within the range of these noble Christian people, of princely means and admirable spirit, they met with such a cordial welcome, such a generous hospitality, such a hearty introduction to multitudes of like-minded followers of Christ, that the time of the delighted travellers flew by on golden wings.

There was only one thing to mar their happiness. The health of Mr. May not having been restored, although improved, and that of Mrs. May having been considerably impaired, it was felt that the duties of a city parish were beyond their strength. So, once again, a resignation of the Rectorship in Philadelphia was sent, and, at the earnest solicitation of Mr. May, was reluctantly accepted by the church in May or June of 1840.

Freed thus from parochial engagement, but without a home, the travellers came back from their long

sojourn abroad, rich in sweet memories, though uncertain as to future settlement.

> "Some natural tears they dropped, but wiped them soon;
>   The world was all before them, where to choose
>   Their place of rest, and Providence their guide."

Attended to the ship in England by the kind
friends whom they had learned most ardently to
love, they landed in New York, November 20, 1840,
and by that night were with dear relatives in Philadelphia.

CHAPTER V.

God never fails the souls that humbly trust him. When informed in England that his thrice offered resignation of St. Paul's had been accepted, Mr. May had written in his journal, "I am now adrift, and must trust the good providence of God to lead me to some safe and happy mooring; may he give me a heart to serve him, and then *the place* where I shall serve, will be of slight account." The very spirit of the record, shows that *the heart* for service was actually his before the prayer. *The place* for it came in its due time. Almost as soon as it was known in the United States that he was disconnected from St. Paul's, offers of other positions were presented. Doubts of his strength for parish duty prevented on his part, an immediate engagement. But when, after a winter at the South, and yet another in retirement, with intermediate testings of his voice, he found sufficient evidences of recovery to warrant entrance upon regular work, he accepted, in July of 1842, the offer of the Professorship of Church History in the Protestant Episcopal Theological Seminary of Virginia. This was the school in which he had commenced his early studies for the ministry. It had grown considerably from its first beginning—had taken up a new position on the heights, three miles from Alexandria, and overlooking Washington—and

6

with enlarged resources, ample buildings, and increasing reputation, was gathering to itself the
greater portion of the students from the most evangelical portion of the Church throughout the Union.

It was the very place for Mr. May. Its distance
from the town entirely suited his always indulged
taste for country life. Its elevated location insured,
for his now somewhat weakened constitution, the
pure airs that he required. Its position between Alexandria and Washington afforded him facilities for
large literary, social, and religious intercourse. And
its comparatively light professorial duties, with only
one Sunday service that he would be bound for, gave
opportunity for gradually recruiting his long over-
tasked and injured voice.

And as the place was just the one for him, so he
was the very person for the place. His thoroughly
sound scholarship and clear views of the Gospel, peculiarly qualified him for instruction. His earnest
and pure piety adapted him for Christian influence
amongst the youthful students for the ministry.
His admirably good judgment made him such a
counsellor as was demanded for settlement of important questions about discipline. And his late long
residence in foreign lands had so enriched both his
memory and taste, as eminently to fit him for the
social intercourse of a Professorship, as well as for
illustration of the History he was to teach.

He entered on his duties in the Fall of 1842, his
Alma Mater conferring on him what he long previously had deserved, the degree of Doctor of Divinity.

His associates at the Seminary were all that he
could wish, Bishop Meade, one of the purest and

most fearless advocates of Gospel truth in the whole
land, was, as Bishop of Virginia, *ex officio* the President; and, though residing elsewhere, spent about a
month of every year in lecturing on Pastoral Theology. Dr. William Sparrow, a noble theologian,
with mental powers of an unusually high order, and
piety that no one possibly could doubt, was in the
chair of Christian Evidences and Divinity. While
in the Professorship of Biblical Interpretation, was
Dr. Joseph Packard, not only accurate and rich in
scholarship, but also " a good man, full of the Holy
Ghost and of faith." To these excellent men, the
two last with Christian families about them, like-
minded and like-hearted with themselves, were
joined, as near neighbors and companions, the Rev.
George A. Smith, of the Clarence Female Seminary,
and the Rev. William N. Pendleton, of the Virginia
High School, both evangelical and faithful ministers. And, some time subsequently, the Rt. Rev.
John Johns, D.D., elected Assistant Bishop of Virginia, after a brief residence in Richmond and Wil-
liamsburg, erected for himself a house on " Seminary Hill," adding his family to its choice society.
A more delightfully harmonious combination of fine
elements could hardly have been found in any
social circle on the globe ; and, of course, with such
companions, all full of the spirit of the Gospel, all
ardently devoted to the cause of Christ, time could
not but pass pleasantly. Then, too, there was much
congenial society, both clerical and lay, in Alexandria, Washington, and Georgetown, as well as in the
adjoining districts of Virginia. And thus the seed
was sown for harvests of enjoyment, which in successive years were fully reaped.

Mrs. May was not able to accompany her husband to the Seminary when he first went there. She remained necessarily in Philadelphia, under medical advice, during the winter, but went to Alexandria the following spring, and spent the latter portion of the Seminary term. In the fall of 1843 she was with Dr. May in the professional mansion on the hill; and then commenced the golden days of her husband's Seminary residence. He had already come to be familiar with his duties, and was prosecuting them with earnest zeal. His presence, added to that of the previous professors, was drawing the attention of students to the school; and, in its general management and progress, all things were proceeding pleasantly. When, therefore, the true help-meet God had given, came to brighten up his dwelling with her presence, his new-found Eden became really a Paradise to his affectionately domestic tastes. He had again, after six years of conscious want, *a home*. And with their European observation of what went to make home pleasant, added to their own personal previous experience, they were together enabled to make home as happy as delicate affection, cheerful piety, cultivated taste, and generous sociality could make it.

The professors and their families, first of all, were made invariably and entirely welcome. A pleasant social intercourse with these, making, as nearly as possible, one Christian family of all, was habitually invited and kept up; and so kind and close became the intimacies thus established, that if one member suffered, all seemed to suffer with it; if one was honored, all obviously rejoiced.

The students, too, found ready entertainment,

alike in the drawing-room and at the table, and were encouraged to feel themselves thoroughly at home. With several, out of almost every class, such influence was gained, that they seemed measurably members of the household, and periodically had their places at family prayers and meals, the effort being to make them understand that they were not mere students, but loved Christian friends. Those who are familiar with the Seminary history, will remember, here, such names as those of Albert Duy, Dudley Tyng, Henry Messenger, Robert Smith, William Bryant, Henry Dennison, and J. A. Shanklin,—names written now in heaven, and fragrant with blessed memories on earth.

Friends, too, from Alexandria, from Washington, from Georgetown, from various other portions of our country, and not unfrequently from foreign lands, came, in successive years, to taste the sweets of Christian fellowship within this happy model dwelling, and never came too numerously or frequently to find warm welcome, cordial entertainment, and every delicate and kind attention that the most cultivated, thorough hospitality could show.

And not the least among the welcomes and the entertainments there, were those extended to the missionaries of the Gospel, either before their departure for their work, or at their coming to recruit themselves anew for it. For the foreign missions of the Protestant Episcopal communion, the Seminary in Virginia was the chief source of supply; and, after the first three that went to Africa, the greater part, both for that mission-field and China, went out from beneath the teachings and influence of Dr. May. Of course, in their history and work as missionaries, such Christians as himself and Mrs. May felt an affectionately earnest interest. When they were about to go forth to their labors, they were expected always to make a visit to "Maywood;" and when they came back, worn out with those labors, to tell what God had wrought among the Gentiles by them, a part at least of the time spent by them in America, was there regularly claimed. No entertainment was thought too generous for those who risked, thus, life or health for Jesus; gave up their home comforts and home friends for his sake; and labored amongst barbarous, unsympathizing people, for the extension of his blessed cause.

Of the cordial feeling with which such were sent forth, some idea may be formed from the following letter to a valued student of the Seminary, who had made up his own mind to go out to Africa, but had feared that his family might possibly oppose his views:

"April 3, 1848.

"MY DEAR FRIEND:

"Mrs. May's heart is full with regard to the most remarkable letter you have sent us from your sister, but her hand is tied from her want of health and strength. She cannot restrain, however, the utterance of what she feels, and so uses my pen. We could not command our nerves to read the letter through at once. What can the grace of God do? Is it possible that a sister, who is so affectionate and tender, can write as she does, to consign you to the will of God? Truly, the Lord shows his power, and we magnify his grace in mother, son, and sister. The tender spirit of your sister is the more remarkable as it is strengthened to sustain what now it bears. We already had loved her for your sake; we now love her for the Lord's sake and for her own. Is it not possible that, in some way, we may have the happiness of seeing her and your mother? We cannot but love them, and in them bless the Lord.

"And have *you* strength, my dear friend, while feeling the power of such ties, to go forth? The Lord God of Abraham, Isaac, and Jacob, our covenant God, whose grace is unsearchable, and whose truth is everlasting rock, go with you. To the love, the exceeding tender love of mother and sister, will be added the love of the Church, and of all that have known you here. The prayers of all will be offered for you and your work. Our gracious God give you strength, and comfort you. It was hard for us at first to give you up; our hearts shrunk back; but now we can say nothing, since mother and sister say, 'God's will be done.' As you are ready not to be bound, only, but to die, if needful, for the name of the Lord Jesus, we would not weep nor break your heart. The richest grace of our most gracious God and Saviour be ever yours. Mrs. May joins in an expression of Christian affection for you as a friend and brother in a common Saviour, and as now to be a *living* sacrifice to him.

"Yours, ever, in Christ,
"JAMES MAY."

And then this, to China, tells how his heart was with the ones that had gone forth to their work, and were laboring in foreign countries for the conversion of the nations:

"THEOLOGICAL SEMINARY,
December 27, 1847.

" MY DEAR FRIEND :

. " You would hardly believe how often, how very often, we have talked of you and your great work, and as often set times for writing to you.   We have not forgotten how you used to be with us, and how welcome and gratifying to us were your visits, as you stood by our triple cannon stove, and told us, with a little shrug, of this and that thing relating to your mission.   About that same stove is still a warm place for not only all our ordinary visitors, but our friends abroad, and especially yourself and yours ; the warm place for these last, being in our hearts as well.

" We rejoice to hear of the Lord's favor to your work.   A great and effectual door seems to be opened to you by his providence, and I trust his Spirit is not wanting.

" My dear brother, I would that I could say a word to aid in strengthening your spirit and that of Mrs. S.   Separated as you are from us by half the circumference of the earth, you have with us a common interest in a covenant God.   His grace is of as full sufficiency in China as in America.   You may be assured of the unimpaired sympathy and love of those whom you have left on these shores ; and God forbid that we should cease to pray for you.   But our sympathy and love, and even prayers, are not your strength.   That standeth in the name of the Lord.   When we regard the vast field of unevangelized nations, and the immense difficulties in the way of subduing the hearts of men to Christ, it seems hopeless to attempt the conversion of the world.

But 'before Zerubabel the great mountain shall become a plain;' for it is 'not by might nor by power, but by my Spirit, saith the Lord of hosts.' With what ease does the Spirit subdue men? To him it is as easy to convert three millions in a day as 'three thousand.' Why is not that Spirit given in the measure needful? Is it because God's covenant forbids? Nay, is not the obstacle in the hearts of Christians? May God prepare the way in these, and then come in great power, to give free course and glory to his word.

"Give warmest love from Mrs. May and self to Mrs. S. (in which *you* have equal share), and to Bishop and Mrs. Boone. Do not make my misdoings an apology for not writing. Anything about your mission or your personal affairs will interest us, even to your cats and mice, if there are such animals among the *celestial* antipodes. Give us a specimen of one day's routine. Omit nothing. Do you eat beef, veal, pork, mutton, and fowls, hams, and potatoes, as we do here? Do you chew with your teeth, like us? If you eat at all, do you eat thrice a day, and then sleep? Or, if you walk at all, do you go on stilts or sabots? Or, in *celestial* regions, do you go in the clouds? Do tell us how it is.

"Your truly affectionate friend,

"JAMES MAY."

And this, to Africa, in even tenderer spirit still:

"THEOLOGICAL SEMINARY,
January 14, 1850.

"REVEREND AND DEAR, VERY DEAR BROTHER:

"We bless the Lord. To him only the praise is due. The Liberia packet brought such good news from you all, that our souls were lifted up in praise. Your letter came to us on the 1st, giving us most eminently a happy New Year. When we read, our hearts were full, and overflowed. To hear that you all were well and happy in your blessed work, and that the Lord is with you, the source of these good things, was too much for our hard hearts to resist. We yielded, gave vent to our emotions, and wished we were among you. Blessed be the Lord our God. And blessings rich and many from his hand be on you and the brethren with you, now and evermore.

" Well, my dear brother, you have tried the work in Africa, and found it good, and you are happy in the midst of it. This is gladdening indeed. Be still strong in the Lord, brother, and as you have grace, strengthen the brethren. I trust we may be strengthened together with you. We have as much need of your prayers as you can have of ours. May the Spirit given you be multiplied by being given to us also.

" Your account of your surveying the ocean to get a sight of the expected sail, interested us greatly. May your eyes be often gladdened by such an object.

" Whatever you can say to us about your movements, labors, fellow-laborers, and pupils, will interest us, and the more detail the better."

Then, after long details of news, " Our warmest love for Brother Payne and his true-hearted wife. I bless them in the name of the Lord, and bless the Lord for them. Assure them that we love them. Mrs. May joins in warmest Christian love to you.

" As ever, and may it be evermore, your affectionate brother,

" JAMES MAY."

And, still later:

" I am mightily drawn towards your female associates. Some I love from sight; for your own jewel, and Brother Hening's, I have seen. Then Mrs. Payne, (I must always stop to bless the admirable wife and missionary sister), I have formed a high opinion of. Her letters, her spirit, her readiness to make sacrifices, commend her to our judgments and our hearts. Miss Williford we have become acquainted with through the letters from Africa. Go directly to her, take her by the hand, bid her God speed in our name, and give her our Christian and fraternal love. Give her a good nosegay. I wish we could drop into it an American rose, a lily, and a jessamine, all with our cards."

And then, what interest was felt in news from them, may be seen from this to the beloved Hoffman, at Cape Palmas:

" THEOLOGICAL SEMINARY,
April 19, 1853.

" MY DEAR BROTHER HOFFMAN:

" I send you and Mrs. Hoffman, and all our brethren and sisters in Africa, greeting. We rejoice at the last intelligence we had of you by Brother Rambo. ' Good news from a far country is like cold water to a thirsty soul.' We drank, and were refreshed. But our thirst is renewed. We desire to hear more. We multiplied the questions to Brother Rambo very diligently. We inquired about you all, about your pupils, Christian villagers, and the whole Grebo tribe; and extended our inquiries about matters all along the coast, and some distance into the interior,—as far, at least, as Brother Rambo

had travelled. Then, after a time, Brother Smith*
had letters from Brother Scott and wife, who had
reached Monrovia safely and in good hopes. After
Brother Rambo's visit, Mr. and Mrs. Hening, with
their daughter, passed two or three weeks with us,
Brother Hening delivering us most admirable addresses in the Chapel. Last week, most unexpect-
edly, came Bishop Boone, with a native Chinese
candidate for orders, Mr. Tong, the latter in full
native costume, a very interesting and intelligent
young man. Both made addresses to the students.

"After mentioning these facts, I must tell you
more particularly of a feast that we have had. Do
not suspect me of any desertion of the temperance
cause, when I write of *a grand wine drinking*, kept up
for weeks. It began at a tea-table. Brother Rambo
arrived at our door just before tea on a Friday evening. He had hardly been seated in my study, when,
on looking out at the window, I discerned the figure
of a very *fraternal*-looking person toiling up the hill,
towards our door. When I saw him put hand to
our gate, as if making his way to our parlor, I went
to the study door, and lo, it was Brother Callaway,
just arrived from Kansas. I called, ' Come, brother,
this is the right way, and here is the man you will
delight to meet.' And such delight! Such shaking
of hands! Such greeting! How can I tell of it? We
did everything but kiss, and, but that such mode of
holy greeting has passed away, we should probably
have fallen into it. Then came in Mrs. May, and
so more and long shaking of hands, and expressions

---

* R. Smith, who subsequently went to Africa himself, and
died there.

of joy and welcome. After a little, the tea-bell rang, and we all went down, and then began the wine-drinking. I ought to have said that Brothers Smith and Wright, candidates for Africa, came also in to tea. We all sat around the table, and all drank the wine from one cup, and that cup Mr. Rambo ministered. Such, questioning! Such calling for more and more! Brother Rambo, however, served us well. Dear brother! he was a little excited, his nerves showed it. And there was good Brother Callaway, he could not eat; and Brothers Smith and Wright, too, lost their appetites. But we continued to drink the wine, which Brother Rambo continued to pour out.

"After tea, we pushed our chairs back, and sang 'Rock of Ages,' and Brother Rambo prayed. I saw no proof of intoxication, except some little reddening and watering of the eyes.

"We kept the thing up after we were well started; for, after Brother Rambo left us, came Mr. and Mrs. Hening. They ministered more of the same wine, and kept our cup full. Then Bishop Boone ministered the same. It occurred to us that whether Brothers Rambo and Hening ministered wine from Africa, or Bishop Boone from Asia, it had the same taste. Dear Brother Hoffman, it savored, we think, of the wine of Eshcol, at any rate, of the promised land. It was most precious. It refreshed, strengthened, cheered and gladdened us. We would have yet more of the same."

The little bit of playful *badinage* which follows this is too pleasant to be here omitted, illustrating, as it does, the genial spirit and quaint humor habitually indulged in his intercourse with chosen friends, though little suspected by more distant ones:

"I give you a diagram of our feasting table when we drank the wine, as before described. . . . The important post, No. 1, was occupied by one of the class of beings such as, in Africa, are called 'angels.' My house is blessed with one, to whom we give the place of honor. In America, I may remark, we do not generally call such beings 'angels.' With us, they are not quite so etherial as yours may be. Ours appear among us in corporeal form, very lovely and very comforting, but still not aërial nor winged. When we speak affectionately, we call them 'dear;' when with admiration 'the fair;' when with forbearing kindness, 'weaker vessels,' but not 'angels.' Our desires are great (do not condemn our curiosity) to see those happy angels in Africa who cheer your tables and animate your domestic circles. Without being willing to bend a knee before them, or make any sign of adoration, I should be happy (if it were not presumptuous) to reach forth my hand to them for a salutation. Our 'fair' ones here smile very sweetly on us (I mean such of us as are favored in our approaches), and we offer them flowers, and by many delicate acts and services endeavor to make sure of their good graces. Just now we have the arbutus from our woods; and though we would not dare to reach up to your ways, in Africa, of preparing and presenting tropical bouquets, we try to do according to our measure. Do not despise our humble imitations.

"My dear brother, we do not envy you your blessings and your joys. We would they were multiplied a hundred fold. Your sweet and cheering associates, those angels, and your flowers,—do enjoy them to the full. We pray that you may be blessed, also, with a presence which may ever stay you with *divine* aid and comfort. Go on your way, and fulfil your work cheerfully and hopefully. Do not always walk in valleys and under clouds. Go sometimes to the top of Pisgah, and look away into the Promised Land. You have even now a foretaste of the precious fruits of the Upper Canaan. Some grapes of Eshcol are brought, and the good wine I spoke of. Let us taste, drink, be cheered, take up staff and scrip, and go onward. Hard hearts, blind and dull understandings, you may find among your native pupils. But sow patiently. The harvest shall come, through the power and riches of the grace of Christ. Do not faint; in due season you shall reap.

"Your affectionate brother,

"JAMES MAY."

No wonder that Mr. Hoffman should have said, on transmitting this and other kindred ones, "No letters ever comforted me more than these of the dear departed one—so cheerful, so warm from his very heart of hearts!" And no wonder, that, with such a spirit in the Seminary, the missionary zeal amongst the students should have been always fresh and ardent, and a constant flow of laborers for the work have met the constantly recurring call for them.

The domestic "angel" of his household was not slow to aid in these his efforts to sustain the hearts of missionaries. She loved them for their work's sake, and for Jesus' sake, as he did—rejoiced to bid them "God speed" at their departure, and cordial welcome upon their return—devised and executed plans which sometimes brought in large sums for the missions*—and when, at one time, there was questioning what should be done with a young native African, sent over to this country to be educated for the ministry, she, with Dr. May, threw open their own home to him, boarded and clothed him without any thought of compensation, and, with the aid of some among the students, affectionately and considerately trained him for his work. As he was returning to his place in Africa, she wrote to Mr. Hoffman, who was to take him to his transatlantic home:

"MAYWOOD, February 16, 1849.

" MY DEAR FRIEND :

" *Musu* is about to leave us, and I cannot let him go without a message to you. Allow me to express, what I am sure you already know, our cordial and heartfelt interest and sympathy, in reference to the great work to which you have devoted your life.

" And I would ask, as a special favor, that you would allow us to aid you in any plans you may form for the good of the poor, benighted Africans. Both Dr. May and myself, as well as my sister M., will esteem it a kindness to be thus employed. If you have another Musu to send to us, be assured he shall be welcomed for his Master's sake, for yours, and for his own. It would indeed be an honor to aid, by the smallest effort, in bringing on that glorious day, when ' the knowledge of the Lord shall cover the earth, as the waters cover the sea.'

" And now, dear Christian friend and brother, to

---

* $800 were thus raised in one case for a school in Africa.

the watchful care, the unfailing kindness, the tender sympathy of our covenant God, I would most affectionately commend you. May he guard you from the dangers of the deep, and bring you in safety to the haven where you would be. And most earnestly we will pray that he may bless abundantly every effort you may make for the promotion of his glory. May I ask that you will sometimes remember us in your prayers, and believe me to be, with the sincerity of Christian regard,

"Truly your friend,
"Ellen S. May."

One other letter merits an insertion here, alike for its historic interest and the light it sheds on the general missionary feeling at the Seminary. It is descriptive of the consecration of the Rev. John Payne, D.D., as Bishop of Cape Palmas, on the coast of Africa.

"Theological Seminary,
July 13th, 1851.

" My dear Sister :

" We have had a good time. You ought to have been here and had your tabernacle; we said often, how sister M. would have enjoyed it.

" As soon as we heard of Dr. Payne's arrival in Baltimore, I mounted and went off to Alexandria, and sent notices by mail and telegraph to Boston, New York, Philadelphia, Baltimore, Washington, Richmond, Petersburg, and Charleston. Bishop Meade, who was on a visitation in the country, had requested us not to wait to hear from him; and in order to have the consecration in our examination week, no time was to be lost. It was a moment of

great interest when news of Dr. Payne having
landed reached us.   There was quite a buzz in the
Seminary.   On Saturday, the 5th, Dr. Payne and a
new Grebo brother in Christ * (who in his native
tongue is named *Wah*, in English, G. T. Bedell) arrived at our door.   Our arms were wide and our
hearts wider.   We could have given a good embrace
to the Grebo with Brother Payne.   Then, to see
Siah's greeting!   How he shook hands, and showed
his beautiful native ivory.   *Wah* and he were ac-
quaintances from childhood, and indeed distantly
related to each other.   Brother Payne stayed with
us till last Friday,—nearly a week.   We talked all
the time, and got our hearts so wound round the
mission, and the brothers and sisters there, that I
doubt whether we shall get loose again.   Dr. Payne
preached for us twice on Sunday, the 6th, and at
night gave an intensely interesting account of the
missions on the coast of Africa.   But *the great day*
was Thursday.   In the morning (the examination
being over), Messrs. Hawkins, Hubbard, Leacock,
were ordained deacons in our chapel, and Messrs.
Callaway and Keith, priests.   Mr. Bedell, from New
York, preached the ordination sermon, a most
admirable discourse in all respects.   The occasion
brought together a large number of our alumni.
In the afternoon, just after the diplomas were given,
Dr. Payne, as previously announced, made an address to the students and alumni, and a large congregation.   It was a history of his missionary life.

* This was a third native African brought over to be educated
for the ministry, as Musu had been. *Siah*, a second, had been
for some time an inmate at the house of Dr. May, under training
for his work.

He spoke of his connection with the Seminary, which he called his Antioch, and alluded to those once joined with him, who are now in the heavenly Sanctuary. The Spirit was powerful in his words; all hearts were touched. A brother told me, afterwards, that he could not restrain his tears, and feared lest he might be alone in his feelings, till he heard sobs all around. He looked to Mr. Dalrymple, who sat in the chancel (having offered prayers), and saw him bury his face in the sleeves of his surplice. We did cry outright, and have hardly done crying yet.

"On Friday I took Dr. Payne to Alexandria before breakfast, to be ready for the consecration. A large congregation met in St. Paul's Church, of clergymen and others, at 11 o'clock. And what a scene! There were four Bishops (Meade, Johns, Eastburn, and Lee), a committee of the Missionary Board from New York (Dr. Tyng, Mr. Bedell, and Mr. Cooke), and many others from distant places. There stood up, in a surplice, at the desk, the majestic figure of Dr. Bull, and by his side Dr. Tyng, who were to read the service. Outside of the chancel, in the aisle, sat the well-beloved Bishop-elect. How we blessed and prayed for him! Up in the gallery, over against the pulpit, were our two Grebo brothers, witnesses for Africa and the mission. Their faces seemed to shine as they looked on. When the services were over, we greeted the Missionary Bishop, and bade him God speed right heartily.

"At 5 P.M. there was a missionary meeting, and addresses were made by Bishop Payne, Mr. Nelson (missionary to China), and Dr. Tyng. A good spirit was there. Now all is over. Bishop Payne went off on Saturday to Washington, to spend Sunday, and was to go thence to Baltimore. He will spend the winter in the West and South, and return to us in the spring, when he expects to go back to his African home. That African home he described in one of his addresses as three hundred yards from the sea-beach, surrounded by cocoa trees and beautiful flowers, and opening on one side to the ocean. There he expects to pass his life. Mrs. Payne is not with him; her health was good, and did not require her to leave home. She suffers, too, dreadfully upon the sea. But, above all, duty to the mission called her to stay there. All the missionaries but herself being young in the work, and some of them not acclimated, she thought she ought not to leave them.

"Mrs. Hoffman fulfils all their expectations. She is cheerful, devoted, and of sound judgment. Bishop Payne thinks her uniform cheerfulness and happiness of temper greatly favor her health in that climate.

"Your affectionate brother,
"JAMES MAY."

Nor was it missions to the heathen only, that engaged attention thus. Missions were organized by the students at the Seminary, for the sailors in the port of Alexandria, for criminals and slaves confined there in the jail, and for every poor country neighborhood for miles around. And to all such efforts to evangelize the region, Dr. May lent always his most hearty aid,—often accompanied the students to their "stations,"—preached, as he had done in his mission school-houses around Wilkesbarre, searching, straightforward, simple addresses to the heart—not failing, ere he left, to take each humble hearer by the hand and address to him some words of friendly interest. And if a clergyman in either of the neighboring towns, or any of the various country churches within reach, required assistance, no winter wind or summer sun kept Dr. May from answering the call for it, if his engagements at the Seminary did not hinder. Mere personal discomfort never seemed to be considered, where opportunities were thus presented of doing something for the extension of Christ's Gospel, or for the help of a burdened brother, in his need.

To keep alive among the students the missionary spirit he thus cherished, a monthly meeting was held regularly at the Seminary, of which he was the ordinary president. At this was read intelligence from every quarter of the world relating to the progress of the cause of the Redeemer, prayers were presented for the missionaries in the field, and correspondence with other like organizations sometimes offered. Letters from missionaries, both in foreign and domestic service, came in to animate the exercises; and addresses from such as were either going forth to labor, or had come home to recruit, were secured as frequently as possible.

A society for rhetorical and intellectual improvement had Dr. May also for its president, and held its meetings every week.

And still another thing, with which those familiar with the Seminary will most pleasantly connect his memory, was what might be called *the* meeting of the institution. This was a gathering of all the students, presided over by the officers of the Seminary in rotation; held every Thursday evening; addressed by the several professors present, and known as "the faculty meeting," from this cause. The special object of it was to cultivate among the students the earnest, practical, and loving piety becoming those who were preparing for the ministry. The clear intellect of Dr. Sparrow, the Biblical learning of Dr. Packard, and the pure holiness and ministerial experience of Dr. May, found here appropriate and beautiful expression, combined themselves for the improvement of the young men beneath their charge, and poured forth such a Pactolœan stream of rich instruction, that few could fail to gather up some golden grains. Not a small number of the former students of the Seminary look back to that weekly meeting as one of the greatest of the privileges of their lives; and feel that in the doctrinal, experimental, practical addresses there delivered, more useful preparation for their ministerial work was gained, than even in the exercises of the lecture and class-rooms.

In 1851, an association for the improvement of the grounds and buildings of the Seminary was inaugurated, and to this Dr. May lent cordially his efforts, with his accustomed zeal and energy. The issue of its operations, aided greatly by his correspondence and exertions, was a great beautifying of the grounds about the Institution, and, gradually, of entirely new and noble buildings for its use. Of these, " St. George's Hall " was erected through a gift of $5000 from members of St. George's Church, New York, under the pastorate of the Rev. Dr. Tyng; " Aspinwall Hall," through one of $20,000 from W. H. Aspinwall, Esq., of Ascension Church, New

York, under the pastorate of the Rev. G. T. Bedell; " *Meade Hall*," a wing to this, through a fund of $10,000, given or raised by the Alumni of the Seminary; and " *Bohlen Hall*," another wing, through a contribution of $10,000 from John Bohlen, Esq., and sister, Philadelphia, these last two donors having previously united equally with Bishop Meade in the erection of a handsome building for the Library, at a cost of $8000. The new buildings all were finished, as to their exterior, and most of them in use, before the close of 1860, forming, in their substantially elegant entireness, a glorious crown for the Seminary Hill, and an apparently enduring scene of noble Christian education for the ministry. Their completion, to which Dr. May and his ever earnest wife contributed much by their exertions, seemed to him the culminating point of his happy residence of nineteen years at the Seminary of Virginia. It proved to be such. The brief remaining period of his continuance there had broad shadows thrown across its sunshine, and went gradually down towards night.

The health of Mrs. May had been impaired by the fatigues of their European journeys, and from thenceforward she had often been subjected to much suffering. None would have suspected it who saw her cheerfulness in company, or listened to the ringing laugh that burst forth freely at a sally from a friend. But still the suffering deepened gradually in intensity, and by the time that the first of the new buildings drew near completion, she had to leave their pleasant home upon the hill, and give herself entirely up to medical care in Philadelphia and

Lancaster.* But no skill could stay the progress of disease, which now was evidently deeply seated in her system. Slowly, but steadily, amidst pains amounting oftentimes to agony, her once vigorous strength declined, though still her cheerful spirit and her humble trust in Christ shed constant brightness round her. Her husband spent with her all the time that could be spared from his duties at the Seminary; kept up an affectionate daily correspondence in the intervals; and hoped, though the hope grew gradually fainter, that God might yet restore her fully to him. But at the winter vacation of 1860–61, while visiting together different friends in Philadelphia, a sudden access of disease became alarming; anguishing pain, defying every remedy, came on; consciousness rapidly gave way; and on the 10th of January, 1861, her earnest, loving, beautiful, and holy Christian life drew to its close. With only power to speak one word expressive of her still

---

* The following letter refers sadly to this period:

"Mrs. May has been called to suffer. After I left her in Lancaster, I had such bad reports of her case, that I went back for a few days. I left her somewhat better, and the Doctor flatters us with the hope of relief.

"I am a boarder at the Seminary table, and a lodger at my own lonely house. My quiet is not broken except by the tick of the clock, making a hollow sound in my empty room. I cannot say when Mrs. May will be able to join me. Certainly not before Christmas. All depends on her health. I have been tried, sorely tried; but I trust the peaceable fruits of righteousness may follow. I know I have had some profitable experience. I see more clearly the truth of God's word. I am disposed to trust it more simply. Oh! that I could teach, preach, and live the Gospel more effectually. I fear we are not as fully committed to it as we ought to be. Is it not a fire and a hammer that breaketh the rock in pieces?"

strong faith in Christ, she passed from the society of earth to that of heaven,—went to be with her Saviour,—and her husband was alone.

So closely had the life of Dr. May been intertwined with that of Mrs. May, that it was hardly thought by friends he could survive the breakage of the ties which bound her to him. Indeed, it did appear, at first, as if he, too, must needs be swept off by the blast that carried her away from him to eternity. He said, subsequently, "Oh! what a storm of suffering rose in her last days. I myself was carried away by its violence in a sort of delirium, not knowing where I was." But God, according to his gracious promise of strength proportioned to the exigencies of the day, gave him such comfort, in the tender sympathy of friends, as well as from his Christian faith and hope, as enabled him to stand the shock of his bereavement; lifted his eye to the rest his wife had reached; pointed him forward to the glad reunion to be hoped for; and induced unselfish rejoicing at her gain, even though feeling unto agony his own irreparable loss. His own words were, in view of the condition of the country at the time, "Whatever dangers or disasters may hang over us who live, the Divine Guardian has taken her into a safe shelter, and so I am comforted." "Tears for the departed may be those of tenderness, as well as of distress. I trust I do say, 'it is well with her,' and, so far as the gracious purposes of God are concerned in the separation, 'it is well with the survivor.' But sorrow may fill the heart even where faith and hope prevail, for there is a sorrow which is not without hope." Thus strengthened by the Spirit, he meekly bowed his will to the Divine; checked all

undue indulgence of his grief; went back, within
a fortnight, to his solitary dwelling; and, while
every object reminded him of the beloved dead,
braced himself resolutely for his still remaining
duties to the living.*

But the discipline of trial was not ended yet. The
clouds returned after the rain. While the pain of
one great grief was yet fresh in his bosom, the
threatenings of another, scarcely less afflictive, began
to gather round. On the 20th of December, 1860,
twenty days before the death of Mrs. May, South
Carolina passed her ordinance of secession from the
Union. The revolutionary feeling, of which this
was the token, swept, like a tornado, through the
whole slaveholding South; involved rapidly within
its vortex all the States along the Gulf; thence, turning, spread up the Atlantic coast; and almost before
the tears upon the grave of his departed wife were
dry, Dr. May found himself surrounded with the
signs of an approaching war. The pickets of the
insurrectionary South were pushed up to the lower
shore of the Potomac; the drum-beat of opposing
Union forces was heard from camps upon the other

---

* To an intimate and valued friend he wrote, January 26th:

"Annie W. (a niece) came with me from Philadelphia. We
entered in silence my now desolate house. There was no voice;
but every door, and room, and article of furniture, had a meaning.

"My dear friend, I do now feel solitary. I have awaked to
my loneliness. I did not realize, till now, how much I leaned on
her, and how much I owed to her. Her sagacity, discernment,
and sound judgment, were immeasurably important to me. Yet
I remember that the Lord is ever present. He does at times
answer 'by *terrible* things in righteousness.' But I know his
throne is a mercy-seat, and that we may draw nigh in full assurance of faith."

side; and everything appeared to indicate that immediately around the Fairfax Semiuary would occur the first great field-fight of our fearful civil strife. A further continuance of the exercises of the Seminary became, in such circumstances, dangerous, if not impossible. With heavy hearts, the Northern students were dismissed,—the Southern shortly following; with heavier, hasty arrangements were inaugurated for the breaking up of professorial homes; and when the Union troops, in May of '61, crossed the Potomac, for the occupation of Alexandria and the Virginia Heights, they found the halls and houses on the hill vacant, and ready for their use. The former became a hospital for soldiers; the latter were appropriated as quarters for their officers; and in the rooms where Dr. May and wife had lived so happily for nearly twenty years, the Medical Department of " the Seminary Hospital" set up its shelves.

He never returned there, even to look after his effects, and rescue what remained of them. The recollections of the agitating, painful last hours spent amidst the scenes of former happiness, were too sad for him to be willing to renew them. His furniture, three hundred volumes of his library, many interesting gatherings of their European tour, and even portraits of himself and wife that hung upon the walls, were thus left to the spoiler. And all know what becomes of things abandoned thus, where armies move.

CHAPTER VI.

WHITHER to turn, when thus the floods of civil
conflict rose, was, of course, a question that had
needed rapid settlement from Mr. May. His col-
leagues at the Seminary, swept by the influences of
the hour, were floating Southward. Should he drift
with them? The principles and feelings of a lifetime all said, No. His nineteen years of Southern
residence had not affected in the least his early
views.

The training of his childhood had made slavery
distasteful to him. Long contact with it had left
that distaste unremoved. He never lent the institution any voluntary countenance;* and though content to dwell amidst it quietly, as long as it might
be protected by the laws, he could not find it in his
heart to take its side, when, freely casting off that
shield, it undertook to do battle for its life.

He had always, too, been a devoted "Union
man;" and while he loved the people of the South,
enjoyed their hospitality, was grateful for their kindness to him, and in the Christian fellowship of many
of them found a pure delight, he could not possibly

---

* In all his nineteen Seminary years, great as was sometimes
the difficulty of obtaining "help," he would not *own*, nor, if he
possibly could help it, *hire* a slave.

assent to their ideas as to the independent sovereignty of States. He held that, though a child of
Pennsylvania, and a dweller in Virginia, he was a
citizen of the United States, bound loyally to follow
the great central Government, in preference to that
of any minor part. And, painful as might be the
severance of social ties that had united him to valued
Southern friends, he could not doubt that when the
South seceded from the Union, he was called by his
duty as a citizen to secede from the South.

When, therefore, he perceived the advances of
secession, he gathered gradually about him such
fragments of his worldly substance as he could, and
prepared for what he saw was likely soon to come,
his own departure for the North. Just before hearing of the ordinance of the Virginia Convention,
passed April 17, he wrote to Philadelphia, "I do
not think of going on at once, but wait a little, to see
how affairs will turn. I confess, the sad state of matters in the country spoils my sleep. I wake in the
night, and cannot quiet myself again." And again,
about the same time, "I have just now come from
a lonely walk up the road beyond the High School.
In looking out on the beautiful landscape, now sweet
and lovely in the youth of the year, I cannot but
ask, is it to be polluted with blood, the blood of
civil and fraternal strife? The good Lord deliver
us! Yet we have called upon ourselves righteous
judgments, and have reason to be humbled and to
mourn."

On the 2d of May, he wrote, "I sent by Adams's
Express, to-day, my valise to Philadelphia. The clerk
told me it would have to be transported from Annapo-

lis Junction to Havre-de-Grace (80 miles) by wagon.*
I sent it in order to leave myself as light baggage as
possible, because I know not what difficulties I may
find on my way. The families at the Seminary are
all about to scatter. Many of the students are becoming restless. If they go off, we must suspend.
A few days will settle the matter. You all ask, why
do I not leave? *Simply because I do not think I ought
to be the direct occasion of injury to the Seminary with
which I have been so long connected.* I may never see
it again, for who can tell what destruction may come!
I took tea with Mrs. Packard, this evening, and then
bade farewell. Her tears fell heavily, and so did
those of all."

The next day, the prospect of a speedy close led
him to add, " Many of the students that have held
fast hitherto, are now packing up, and getting ready
for departure. The matron talks of going, on Monday next, to Pennsylvania. If she goes, we must wind
up, and the question of the Seminary will be settled.
Shall we ever reassemble ? Shall we, who now separate, ever meet again this side of death? You can
imagine nothing so sweet and lovely as everything
in nature looks. The new buildings are all just com-
pleted, the last work of the plasterers having been
done last week.† And they are now set off by a
thoroughly cleaned yard, all beautifully green, trees
in young leaf, with numberless flowers and blossoms.
The woods have been raked over and trimmed, and
look as neat as a garden. The birds seem wild with

---

* The railroad bridges between Baltimore and Havre-de-Grace
having been burned April 19.

† *I. e.*, on Meade Hall, the east wing, the rest having been
finished for some time.

delight, and fill the air with song. Who knows how
soon everything here may be destroyed? Though
the buildings and other outside improvements may
remain, the spirit that has filled them may be wanting. The wishes, hopes and aims of those who
founded and sustained the Seminary, are frustrated.
We must, however, leave all with the Lord. All
Mr. Packard's family, except himself, a son, and
cook, went off this morning. Bishop Johns's children started, also, for their sister's, in Amelia. Mrs.
Sparrow and F. may stay until next week. Poor
Dr. S. is pressed down in heart. He mourns for his
country, for the Seminary, for his family, and oh,
how deeply, for the dear afflicted one! If the tears
shed on this hill, this week, were gathered, what an
amount would appear! And yet, is not this but *the
beginning* of sorrows?"

The next we hear of him, he was on his way to
Philadelphia, and the lengthened Southern residence
was at an end.

He bore a heavy heart away with him. The home
he was forsaking in such painful circumstances had
been, deservedly, extremely dear. It was pleasant
in its outward aspect, trees throwing their shadows
on its roof, flowers blooming on its walls, and
birds flitting and singing round its windows. It
had been hallowed by the daily prayers and services
of almost half an ordinary life. It was full of pleasant memories of the students he had taught, the
brethren he had been associated with, the missionaries he had welcomed, and the many friends that he
had entertained. All that his moderate means would
warrant of classic art, of simple elegance, of literary
apparatus, and of domestic comfort, had been gathered

in it. And there was no prospect for him of another like it upon earth. He was too far advanced in life, by this time, to have the hope of setting up another tabernacle, if even he had the heart to do so. To all appearance, he was going off, to be a stranger and sojourner from thenceforth.

And yet, in God's good providence, this sad upbreaking was probably for his eventual good. Had even the Seminary been continued, the home, without the wife in it, must needs have been a perpetual reminder of her absence from him, and his loss. He had written from it, but a little while before he left, "I do feel lonely. I cannot forget that last night, from nine o'clock of January 9th to 2 A.M. of the 10th; that face, so changed; the last looks in silence; and now, the sealed lips in the grave. I find here kind friends, exceedingly kind. But how many things, in the house and out, remind me of the departed,— the furniture of the rooms, the arrangement of it, her handwriting on paper, and various memoranda. Then the aspect of things outside, especially as spring opens, all contribute to keep alive the memory of what can never be again. Sometimes the pressure seems too great to be endured."

Better to leave, than to continue in, a home whose silent chambers thus constantly reminded him of the beloved dead. For though he had precious Christian comfort in his loss; knew where his wife was gone; knew what a blessedness she was enjoying; knew what a happy meeting with her he might hope for; the felt want of her society in scenes which her sweet fellowship had rendered bright, must have made long continuance there unbearable at last.

In Philadelphia, where he arrived May 9th, he

met a cordial welcome. Friends that well knew his excellence, and loved him for his worth, rejoiced to have him with them once again. And, almost immediately, work accordant with his tastes was opened to him. An humble parish at Providence, in the Valley of the Perkiomen, not very distant from his early home, was then without a minister. A member of the family on which it was dependent for its services, met with Dr. May directly after his arrival in the city, and at once engaged him to go up and spend a Sunday there. The visit proved a pleasant one to him and all, and led to others. And though the field was very small, and the salary proportionately so, he eventually became the pastor of the flock there gathered. On the 18th of June, we find him writing from West Chester to the friend that first invited him, " Since my own domestic ties have been broken, and my place in the world has become a lonely one, the kindness of friends outside of my own empty house has become more valuable to me than ever. Where I find sympathy, my gratitude and tenderness bind me. I would be, too, where the Lord is ; and I believe him to be with you.

" If I can, on my visits to your house, be the means of benefit in the way of preaching the Gospel to your neighbors, the pleasure of association with your family will be the greater on that account. Where there is a simple mind for the reception of the word of God, the happiness of making it known is, of course, the more decided."

Again, on the 8th of July, he writes from Philadelphia, " I keep in most pleasant remembrance my visits to your house, and the opportunities there given me for witnessing to the Gospel of Christ.

When I accepted your first invitation to pass a Sunday with you, I supposed that the services of one day would fill up the vacancy in the parish, and that the place would then be supplied by some one, who, as settled pastor, could regularly minister to the people. And now, behold, I have been with you not merely a duality, but a plurality, of Sundays. Several considerations have moved me (shall I say tempted me?) to return thus to your interesting* people. There seemed to be an opportunity of saying something for the Master's cause to a people ready to hear. No engagement of a more imperative kind called me elsewhere. This door seemed to be opened before me in a most unlooked-for way. And, then, to my own feelings (suffering from a wound which the hand of Providence had inflicted, the deepest and sorest of my whole life), I have found a soothing influence in the quietness of the country, and in the Christian associations and sympathy of your household.

"I am tempted to wander from the line of my letter. I meant only to record my remembrance of your school-room and Sunday-school, of the evening services, and of all that appertains to your establishment. I am sure that while you are dedicating all to God, he will overshadow all with his blessing."

The little flock thus taken under his instruction, he continued to look after to the last. Residing still in Philadelphia, with nephews and nieces that had

---

* "Interesting," not from what most persons would have reckoned elements of interest,—cultivation, refinement, intelligence, and the like; but from what better suited his unfastidious taste,— their honest simplicity, and readiness to receive, with meekness, the engrafted word.

bid him welcome to their home, he spent whatever holidays he could command, amongst the people, and always went up on Saturday in time to see some of them before the Sabbath came. His custom was to ride to Norristown, eighteen miles, upon the railway, and there take the stage for seven miles additional. Then, being on the border of the parish, he would alight, and see as many of the families as possible before he rested for the night. On Sunday morning, service was held in a little place of worship, known as Union Church, before or after which he generally contrived to have a friendly word with almost every one. Then came a hasty dinner, and after it a Sunday-school, in which he took a class of boys; and one that visited it said it was beautiful, indeed, to see the Doctor of Divinity and Professor of Church History sit meekly, in that quiet country school, instructing the plain farmers' boys, their faces bent on his with eager interest, and his beaming with mild benevolence, tender feeling, or playful humor, as he taught. School ended, he would be off along the valley, or up among the hills, to inquire after any that were sick, to comfort any that were sorrowing, or to assist, with friendly guidance, any that were endeavoring to come to Christ. Back to his resting-place again, for brief refreshment; then an evening service in a school-room, and so ended the labors of the day. On Monday he was up in the early morning, often before light, and on his way to Philadelphia, in time to be present at a meeting of the clergy, for devotional exercises and conversation about pastoral work, held in the vestry-room of the Church of the Epiphany, at noon.

Before he had been long in Philadelphia, he was

spoken with in reference to another more important field,*—a professorship in the Pennsylvania Training School for Students of Divinity, which had been in operation under the auspices of Bishop Potter, from the fall of 1857. The matter gradually took definite shape in his appointment as Professor of Church History and Polity, and, *pro tempore*, of Doctrinal Theology. Dr. G. Emlen Hare was already in the school as Professor of Scriptural Interpretation; Dr. John A. Vaughan, of Pastoral Care; Dr. P. Van Pelt, of the Languages of Scripture; and other clergymen of Philadelphia, as instructors in various lines; while Bishop Potter gave his personal attention to exercises in the reading of the Liturgy. Dr. C. M. Butler (who finally succeeded to the Chair of Dr. May) brought, subsequently, his fine mental powers and rich accomplishments, to add to those of all the rest; Dr. Goodwin, Provost of the University of Pennsylvania, became Instructor in the Evidences; and thus was formed a Faculty, such as, for piety, high culture, varied learning, and sound wisdom, probably no merely Diocesan Training School had ever previously secured.

Dr. May commenced his duties at the School in September, 1861; met his classes for instruction five days in every week; held, at the request of Bishop Potter, a devotional meeting for the students, on the Saturdays; and gave the Mondays, after the clerical meeting previously referred to, to visiting and correspondence with his many friends. God's provi-

---

* Overtures were also made to him respecting a connection with St. Ann's Church, Brooklyn, as an associate of the Rev. Dr. Cutler; but the professorship and country parish in conjunction, overbore the city church.

dence had brought his floating bark to what seemed a safe and pleasant anchorage; and while the storms of war swept almost everything to wreck about his old Virginia resting-place, he lay here in such sheltered waters, that he hardly felt the rocking of the waves. With delightful coadjutors, with congenial work, with ample opportunities for usefulness, and with a quiet country parish to retire to for the Sunday, there was promise, once again, of happy life. The Lord had not forgotten, nor forsaken, the faithful servant of his Son. He was fulfilling to him the great promise, "at evening time there shall be light." And when, in 1862, the basis of the Training School was made a broader one, a charter as a Divinity School was gotten for it from the Legislature, Dr. John S. Stone was added to its Faculty, and a charming location was secured for it in Western Philadelphia (a *rus in urbe*, where the birds could sing among the branches), his cup was made as full of the ingredients of comfort as it could be for one that had been so bereaved.

The wound he had sustained in his wife's death was gradually being healed by balm from heaven; but the deep scar still was tender, and sometimes throbbed with pain. He wrote to Dr. Packard, March 16, 1863, "I often feel very solitary. I find kind friends; but who can recall the past, or bring back the departed? I had much conflict in mind before I could agree to remain here, and often fancied it would accord better with my feelings to hide myself in some retired country parish. To some extent I have done so. I have a little corner in the country, where for a year and more I have spent

Sundays, and yet continue to preach to a small hand-ful of hearers."

Sorrow, however, did not make him selfish. He knew too well God's sanctifying purpose in it, to sit down and brood needlessly over his grief. He neither wore a saddened countenance because of it, nor sought to draw attention to it in his intercourse with friends. It only led him to look more upwards, more around,—to dwell more on the rest remaining for God's people,—and to cherish tenderer feeling for those chastened like himself. He sought out sufferers, to speak to them those words of comfort which had supported his own spirit. He sent to distant friends, in their distresses, like words of friendly cheer. An excellent young clergyman, that was laid by from his work, and brought quite near the grave, received from him this message of encouragement and counsel:

"In some aspects it may seem hard that, at your early stage, you should be withdrawn from the service to which you had given yourself for life. But you are in the hands of one wiser than yourself. He knows what is best for you, and best for his own honor. In this time of trial, you are taught in his school who calls us to 'learn of him, for he is meek and lowly in heart.' You have learned his love, grace, sovereignty, and power. You know his cross, his blood, 'which speaketh better things than that of Abel.' You may be, you are, daily sprinkled with that blood. Jesus is, to you, 'wisdom and righteousness, sanctification and redemption.' Think of that most pregnant text, 'He hath made *him* to be sin for us, who knew no sin, that we might be made the righteousness of God in him.' We, sinners;

he, righteousness; he, sin (or a sin-offering) for us; we, righteousness in him. Most precious tidings! Hold fast that truth.

"Jesus is a personal, present, living Saviour, nigh you, even in your heart, by the Holy Ghost, who sheds abroad his love. Cleave to him. Rest on him. Believe, and be sure that he is the Christ, the Son of God, who has the words of eternal life. Brother, hold fast your faith. Know that he, having obtained the victory in his own person, will give you also the victory in yours.

" You have a name and place in 'the blessed company of all faithful people.' The sympathy of brethren will be with you to the end. But you have a better fellowship than that with any earthly brethren. Your fellowship is 'with the Father, and with his Son, Jesus Christ.' Grace, mercy, and peace from God the Father, and from Jesus Christ our Lord, be multiplied to you. The God of Jacob be your God and guide, keep and defend you to the end, and then be your portion forever! So I wish, and so I pray."

A brother professor, too, whose son had died a prisoner of war, the third in fifteen months, was thus remembered: " Your son, Willie! I recollect him as he was, when, with his bright face, he used to pass me on his way to school at Howard, or when he came to my door, or I saw him at your house. His face was always lighted with a smile.

"I tenderly feel for you and his mother and family. I read your letter with tears. What can we say? What, but 'Even so, Father!' We are sorrowfully reminded that this is not our rest. I know how closely our hearts cling to places, possessions, and

friends here, and how hard to loose the grasp. But
God has given some very distinct and painful lessons,
during these late years. Hard, hard, indeed, to receive them! But faith overcometh the world. The
victory is mighty, when achieved; but oh, how hard
the achievement! I have shed more tears within
the last three years than ever before. Now they
seem to be natural, and flow unbidden. ـBut why
talk of my own case? How much sadder that of
you and Mrs. P. Let us, however, learn to sit at
the feet of Jesus, to bear his yoke and burden, yea,
his cross. There we may be comforted, and find his
grace sufficient for us.

"Assure Mrs. P. and daughters of our warmest
sympathy. I say, *ours;* for my nieces desire a very
particular participation in the message."

Many such letters flowed at this time from his
pen; and he became, through them, "a son of consolation" to not a few afflicted souls. One series of
such epistles, written to a sufferer that called forth
an especial sympathy, proved such a precious solace
to him in his sickness, and so greatly brightened for
him his passage to the grave, that, for the benefit of
kindred sufferers, they are inserted as an appendix
to this work.

In other ways, too, he sought to be a comforter.
The discouraged student, or despondent minister,
were soon discerned by his ever watchful eye, and
generally had some affectionately friendly intima-
tion how their difficulties might be met and their
anxieties disposed of. The poor, too, had abundant
tokens of his care. A warm place in his heart was
always kept for them; and often, at some humble fire-
side, the Professor of Theology might have been

found, distributing not gifts alone, but kind attentions, which often go much further than all gifts. And when the nights for weekly services arrived, he would be up, as soon as tea was over, to wend his way, not usually to the greater churches, where wealth sits comfortably in its cushioned ease, but rather to the little outskirt gatherings, where poverty draws timidly near Jesus' messengers, to hear from them the glad tidings of great joy. If asked to speak at such places, he was always ready; nothing pleased him better than to " preach the Gospel to the poor." If not a speaker, he would sit as meekly as the humblest, to receive the message that was meant for them.

No wonder that a spirit so beautifully Christ-like should have attracted notice from the Christian eyes around. Jesus himself has said that " he that humbleth himself shall be exalted." "Good Dr. May" (as friends generally called him), shutting himself up in his little country parish, or in the meetings of the city poor, did not escape thus the admiring gaze of those who love to see the Gospel thoroughly lived up to. And when God took from Pennsylvania her excellent Assistant Bishop, the Rt. Rev. Samuel Bowman, D.D.,* the hearts of many, both of the laity and clergy, turned instantly towards Dr. May as a most fit successor to the office. They knew his purity of spirit, his perfect uprightness of walk, his admirable judgment, his fervent piety, and his entire devotion to Christ's truth; and it was thought that it would be a blessing to the Diocese to send

---

* A brother-in-law of Dr. May, who died suddenly by the wayside, August 3, 1861, as he was on a visitation in the western portion of the State.

out among its parishes so clear a preacher of the Gospel, and so truly excellent and pure a man. *He* did not know about the agitation of the matter, till the Special Convention for the choice of an Assistant Bishop met in October, '61. Then he became aware of it, and wrote to the Rev. Dr. Vaughan the following characteristic note, which shows how the ambition that he used to mourn over in his early journal must have been crushed out.

"1520 PINE STREET, October 23, 1861.

" REVEREND AND DEAR BROTHER:

" I was surprised and distressed by hearing (late last evening) that brethren have thoughts of nominating me for election to the office of Assistant Bishop. Very early wakefulness this morning has given me time for communing with my own heart. I am confirmed in the purpose formed last evening, at the moment of hearing the report, to request that this should not be done. So long as there are diffi-, culties enough on the threshold of the question, I need not refer to those of want of faith and of the Holy Ghost, which lie within.

" As to the Diocese, I have neither the physical nor mental energy which the office demands, and especially in these times, when 'men's hearts are failing them for fear.'

" As to myself personally, temperament, and long indulged taste for private life, and fixed domestic habits, unfit me for a public position. The thought of the cares and responsibilities of the office in question, makes my spirit fail. Besides, the course of Providence (as to me) seems to require, or at least allow, more retirement now than ever. The hand of God has touched me, and made me solitary; and while my delight is still 'to teach and to preach Jesus Christ,' it is in such seclusion as is now given me for Sunday duties. On this last point I should like to speak freely, for my heart is in it. But the occasion does not call for my doing so.

"I have now only to ask of you the favor to see that my name be withdrawn, or, rather, that it be not offered to the Convention.

"Your affectionate friend in Christ,

"JAMES MAY."

Of course this put an end to the thought of nominating him; for although there were some ardent friends, that still insisted upon urging his election, and felt confident of carrying it, the greater part of those who would have voted for it thought that it ought not to be pressed against his will. Another much respected Presbyter, of very eminent qualifications for the post, the Rev. William Bacon Stevens, D.D., was therefore settled on and chosen; and Dr. May was suffered, as he wished, to keep the even tenor of his way.

Beyond the inevitable occasional excitement occurring in a state of civil war, there was no further special agitation of his now usually quiet life, till the fall of 1863. Then a question rose, which deeply interested him. Bishop Hopkins, of Vermont, had published, in the stirring times of 1860, a pamphlet in defence of Slavery, designed to calm the commotion of the public spirit at the North upon that point. When the political elections of 1863 were being prepared for, in Pennsylvania, certain gentlemen upon the Democratic side asked leave of Bishop

Hopkins to reproduce and circulate his pamphlet. He consented, and it was so circulated, to a very large extent, throughout the State. Bishop Potter thought that such a circulation in his Diocese might lead to misconception of the position of the Protestant Episcopal Church upon the subject, if the pamphlet were suffered to go thus abroad unnoticed. Accordingly, a paper was prepared, signed by the Bishop and the greater portion of his clergy, protesting strongly against Bishop Hopkins's views, and against this mode of spreading them. Bishop Hopkins met this with an indignant and severe reply. The controversy excited considerable feeling; and, besides many pieces in the newspapers, several pamphlets, combating the main positions that had been assumed by Bishop Hopkins, were issued. Dr. May took no loud part in the discussion. He was not wont to enter stormily into a debate of any kind. But his feelings in this case were much engaged. His long, close contact with the Slave system of the South, had induced in him much thought upon the theme. As he mused on it, at this time, the fire burned; and at last, in November, 1863, he put forth, anonymously a pamphlet, headed, " *Remarks on Bishop Hopkins's Letter on 'The Bible View of Slavery.'* " It was a clear, calm, forcible review of the arguments of Bishop Hopkins, and went more deeply into the heart of the whole matter than anything else that was published at the time. There was no important point urged in the plea for Slavery, that was not fully met and answered. In language perfectly temperate and courteous (for he could use no other), but burning with a grave and tender earnestness, he spoke out, here, the long-suppressed and bridled

sentiments of his whole life, showing clearly that
the Bishop had assumed great points, requiring to be
proven; had made serious mistakes in his Scriptural
interpretations; had confounded, sadly, the warrant-
able providence of God and unjust acts of man; and
had really gone beyond the leading statesmen of the
South in his advocacy of their cause. And, finally,
speaking of the change in public sentiment which
the war had brought about, or intensified with a
new ardor, he said, " The deep religious convictions
of honest minds (call them fanatical, if you please;
the name does not affect the truth) are not matters
of party or of policy. They arise from unchange-
able elements of our nature, wrought on by eternal
truth. They move onward, slowly it may be, but
with a steadiness and force which yields to no opposition. Persecution gives them the more distinct-
ness and power. Woe to the party that sets itself
against them! When Henry IV of France was, for
political reasons, trying to beat down the honest religious convictions of his subjects in Navarre, Beza
said to him, ' Sire, you strike an anvil which has
worn out many hammers.' "

The publication of this pamphlet was the last
public work of Dr. May. He had been enfeebled
in the summer by a violent attack of ague, while
visiting his still loved friends in Wilkesbarre. A
succession of unusually trying colds during the autumn, with occasional recurrence of the chills, had
kept him weak. And though, as winter came, he
seemed to throw off the debilitating influence, and
regain the freshness of his ordinary health, there
probably was still a condition of the system unfavor-
able to resistance of disease. On Friday evening,

the 11th of December, as he was preparing, with his usual benevolence, although unwell, to hold service for the rector of a distant church in Philadelphia, he was struck with a sudden chill, which he supposed to be a new development of ague; rode home, unfortunately through a moist, penetrating, wintry air; took immediately to his bed, and never rallied. The most skilful medical attendance in the city was invoked by anxious friends; but the disease, which proved to be the spotted fever, a malignant form of typhus, was beyond arrest by any skill of man. And as, according to its usual rule, it settled itself especially upon the brain, he was more or less delirious from the beginning, and apparently unable to appreciate the threatening aspect of his case. When told by the physician that he was extremely ill, he would answer, " Yes, they say so;" but evidently as if it related to some other person than himself. His mind was actively at work, but incoherently, the thoughts evolved being broken and incomplete. Friends still were recognized with his accustomed, gentle smile, and every little act of ordinary courtesy attended to; but efforts to engage in connected conversation were in vain. Even his broken thoughts had reference to something good; fragments of prayers, portions of Scripture promises, directions as to duty, or intimations of the conscientious spirit in which it should be done, forming the staple of them; but friends mourned greatly that, in his case, as in that of Mrs. May, the rich, clear, Scriptural faith which had been cherished, could not give forth an intelligible final utterance. As far as he was personally concerned, however, none such was required. John Newton used to say, " Tell me not how one died, but how he lived." And Dr. May had lived with heaven all about him for so many years, in such intimate communion with it, his life so truly "hidden in Christ with God," that those who stood about his bed were perfectly assured where faith would have reposed and hope have looked, had a clear mind been granted him. They knew what clinging arms would have been thrown around the Cross; what reverent eyes would have been turned to Him who hung on it as our surety; and with what a full and childlike trust the hand of faith would have been laid upon the head of Christ, to transfer to that blessed "Lamb of God" the sins of life, and receive, in merciful return, his righteousness. It was not for the sake of the departing Christian, therefore, that they wanted the outspoken words of faith, but only for their own sake, that their hearts might thus be comforted, and for the Church's sake, that it might have a blessing from his testimony. It was not to be, however. Slowly the lamp of life burnt low, and fitfully the flashes of intelligence shot up from it, till, on Friday A.M., December 18th, not a week from the time when he was taken ill, the faithful servant of the Saviour, without ability to speak to those around him, rested,

> "As one that wraps the drapery of his couch about him,
> And lies down to pleasant dreams."

A momentary struggle,—a gentle stoppage of the breath,—and then "asleep in Jesus," and "forever with the Lord."

Thus ended, for this world, the course of one of the most truly Christian spirits with which God has blessed his Church. And thus went off to heaven a soul that had so washed its robes and made them white in the blood of the Lamb, as to leave no doubt behind it whither it was gone. "I would give all that I am worth," said an excellent Christian, at the funeral, "to have, in my own case, the assurance that I have in his of full and glorious salvation." "He had not far to go to reach the gate," wrote another, in respect to him; "for his conversation was in heaven." "Dear Dr. May," was the testimony of a third, "seemed to me more holy than any one I ever knew."

"More holy!" That was the current conviction, in respect to him, among those that had the fullest opportunities for knowing what his character had been. And that was the secret of the love felt for him, and the reverence cherished, in the wide circle of his friends. Intellectually noble, mentally sublime, it was not claimed that he was, more than many others in the Church. With a naturally vigorous intellect, industriously cultivated and enriched, he stood, in mental elevation, much above the crowd. But that which more particularly marked him was a goodness, piety, and purity that never had been stained with a shadow of reproach; inducing, when he was withdrawn, the general feeling that a bright light was extinguished; that a living exemplification of true Scriptural excellence was lost; and that, if Christ had abler servants left to labor for his cause, none holier remained to link this world to heaven.

He rests beside his wife in the churchyard of St. Mary's Parish, West Philadelphia; and might well have on his tombstone, for an epitaph, what the Bishop said of him in his next address to the Convention: "The Rev. Dr. May, long known and most dearly beloved in Philadelphia and throughout the Diocese, a man of singular purity, meekness, fervor, and force."

When such a Christian passes from us to eternity, we cannot but thank God for the example he has left us. For though, as day-spring dims for us the stars, Christ's coming glory may eclipse all virtues of his saints, these are, at present, reflectors to us of his brightness. We steer our course, to some extent, by their direction. We follow them as they have followed him. And seeing that the Christian graces which they manifested were outflows from the deep eternal fountain in himself, we render praise that through his light in them we see light—

> "Praise that from Earth resulting, as it ought,
> To Earth's acknowledged sovereign, finds at once
> Its only just proprietor in him."

Not for the honor of mere human virtue, therefore, but for the honor of the grace of Christ, we turn now to review the character of him, whose life-story has been briefly written. For such review we depend mainly on the words of one that had such opportunities for knowing him as are afforded by close intimacy and near residence for years, the Rev. Dr. Packard. He writes:

"I am glad to hear that a biography of Dr. May is to be published, for I regard him as a model of what a minister of Christ should be. I can truly say that I have never met with so perfect a human character. In an intimate intercourse with him of twenty years, I cannot remember that I ever saw in him any trace of anger, pride, selfishness, or ambition. Baxter has said that good men are not as good as he once thought they were, but have more imperfections; and that nearer approach and fuller trial makes the best appear more weak and faulty than their admirers at a distance think. Dr. May was an exception to this generally just remark. His character bore close examination, and his example of symmetrical and holy excellence was invaluable to all with whom he came in contact."

True piety was the fairest of the train of graces with which Christ had beautified him by his Spirit. No one could know him intimately, without observing that he had caught much of the spirit of his Saviour, and that his life was fed continually from the great well-spring of eternal life. His prayers,— such prayers! pure utterances of devout emotion, expressive of a holy intimacy with his Lord, showed plainly that his communion with an unseen, but living Saviour, was most constant and confiding. He came before the mercy-seat as one that evidently knew the way to it, rejoiced in the privilege of such approach, and found delight in intercourse with the Redeemer. He seemed to feed upon the very name of Christ, and often said that, as we need daily bread for strengthening the body, so must we have for spiritual nourishment continual communications of that bread of heaven which cometh down and giveth life unto the world.

Sincere humility was another obvious trait. He was singularly free from the uprisings of ambition, seeming to look upon himself as an ordinary preacher, and preferring to preach in the smallest places, and to the smallest congregations. He received calls to different important churches, which would never have been known but through reports of others, as he did not speak of them himself.* He often inculcated it upon his students that they should not be concerned about salary or position; but do their duty quietly in some humble corner of Christ's vineyard, and if it pleased him, he would call them to a wider field. And what he said in this respect, he acted on; never thrusting himself forward, never seeking promotion for himself, but leaving it for God to dispose of him as he would;

> " Content to fill a lowly place,
>   If Christ were glorified."

We have seen, thus, how he could decline a bishopric, and give himself to a quiet country parish in preference to an important city church.

And with his piety and his humility was joined a *pure unworldliness.* His thorough deadness to all anxious care about his circumstances in this present life, was quite remarkable. With full ability to enjoy greatly earthly blessings and comforts, when bestowed on him, he never seemed to give himself the least concern about them—received them thankfully, if God's providence imparted them, but showed no sign of wanting them, if it did not. Although, from circumstances now unknown, his salary at one time was very greatly in arrears, and he was driven

---

* Or if he did speak of them at all, it was to some intimate but far off friend, when giving the details of home life that were desired, as where, reciting to a brother off in China the circumstances of a call to Dr. Sparrow, he writes: "I have had a similar alarm, too, for myself; for I was called to succeed Dr. Stone in Brooklyn. I have thought prudence the better part of valor, and declined. It is said that somewhere in Italy is found *upon a tombstone* this inscription: 'I was well, I wished to be better, and am here.' It is important to know at what point to be satisfied."

to a very close economy, he never either uttered a complaint, or even went to urge a payment. And at another time and place, a treasurer not being wont to pay till called upon, examination showed that upwards of two thousand dollars had run up to the Doctor's credit, for which he had not even asked. So truly, through his close and holy union with his Saviour, had the world been crucified to him and he unto the world.

His *sympathetic spirit*, too, was admirable. Though not demonstrative in manner generally, he possessed a warm and tender heart, and was thus able to become a comforter to many. Much tried himself, especially in later life, first by his own ill health, and then by that of his beloved wife, he learned to feel for others in their trials, and thus to follow him who is a merciful as well as faithful High Priest to us, touched with a feeling of our innocent infirmities, because in all points tried as we are, except in the experience of sin. He could truly say, " *Non ignarus mali, miseris succurrere disco*." Friends that rejoiced felt sure of his rejoicing with them; and those that wept, of his weeping also in their griefs. His soul appeared to spring at once to render comfort to a sufferer. He made the case of such his own. And such as knew him went to him in their troubles, with perfect confidence of finding sympathy and aid.

A graceful and unfailing *Christian courtesy* threw also round all intercourse with him its charm. It was the issue not of education, foreign travel, or desire to please, alone, but, much more, of a humility that never would prefer itself to others—of a charity that never sought "its own"—and of a delicate and tender consideration for men's feelings, that never willingly would do anything to wound.

And yet, with all this, there was *firm decision in respect to principle*. He never delayed doing what he felt to be a duty, and never shrunk from it through fear of consequences. He was no reed, to be shaken by the wind. His views of truth were well settled and defined, and were held to, when embraced, most unchangeably and fixedly. He was a man, who, in the old times of martyrdom, would have gone freely to prison or the stake, before he would have yielded any truth on which he was assured that God had set his seal. Even in the days of his first ministry in Wilkesbarre, when declared Evangelism was still extensively unpopular, he never thought of covering from view the great distinctive features of the Gospel, but taught, with full and manly emphasis, our fall in Adam, our recovery through Christ, our thorough dependence on God's mercy in the Saviour, our need of a complete renewal by the Spirit, and then the perfect freeness of salvation, as Heaven's sovereign gift of grace to all that take Christ to their hearts and trust in him. And always, in his more than thirty years of service, though not obtruding offensively his views, he was prepared to give distinctly and decidedly a reason for the faith which conscientiously he held.

This fixedness of principle gave its color to his preaching. From deep conviction that the doctrines of the Cross form the true nourishment of spiritual life, he was determined to know nothing here but Jesus Christ and him crucified. "The Sun of righteousness" must always be the central luminary in his system—the Cross, the foremost constellation in his

sky. No wish for popular applause could induce
him to withhold his simple, clear, emphatic presentation of salvation through a suffering, divine Redeemer. If people wanted to be treated to an entertainment of splendid rhetoric, or brilliant fancy,
or profound philosophy, they must not go where he
was to officiate. But if they wished to hear of
Christ—Christ undertaking to be surety for our race;
Christ coming to fulfil God's will in saving us;
Christ offering to the law his pure obedience in
place of our own sin; Christ dying, rising, inter-
ceding for us at the mercy-seat, that he might thoroughly complete his saving work; and then Christ
sending down his Spirit to give us individual and
personal interest in his salvation—they had but to
inquire where Dr. May would preach. Indeed, he
was, as preacher, almost the embodiment of Cow-
per's sketch of what a preacher ought to be:

> —— "Simple, grave, sincere;
> In doctrine uncorrupt; in language plain,
> And plain in manner; decent, solemn, chaste,
> And natural in gesture; much impressed
> Himself, as conscious of his awful charge,
> And anxious mainly that the flock he fed
> Should feel it too: affectionate in look,
> And tender in address, as well becomes
> A messenger of grace to guilty men."

The Church needs many such. God grant that
of those coming forward to the ministry, there may
at least be *some*, of such piety, such purity, such
zeal for Christ, and such unselfish devotion to his
cause, as may enable them to take the stand, to
emulate the course, and eventually fill the place of
Dr. May.

REMINISCENCES BY DR. RIDDLE,

PRESIDENT OF JEFFERSON COLLEGE, CANONSBURG.

My acquaintance with James May began in the autumn of 1822, the beginning of the collegiate year. Dr. Matthew Brown had been chosen President in September of that year. I had been in college one session, (then of five months). May and I formed part of the first senior class, taught by that well-known preceptor. We were friends almost from our first acquaintance. There was, to me, something attractive, I might say, fascinating, in his first appearance. A shade of sadness, almost melancholy, hung over his finely developed features, as if he had felt some secret sorrow, or experienced some great disappointment. I soon discovered, too, a very marked tendency to the romantic or imaginative in his composition. This, of course, was an additional source of attraction to one of similar age and tendencies. We had read and delighted in many of the books which were my favorites in boyhood. One poem, especially, I remember, was his special pet, "Gertrude of Wyoming." The scenery and the story seemed never to pall upon him. I can recall, even after forty years, how his large eye would dilate, and his voice tremble with emotion, in reciting some of his favorite passages.

He had fine taste for scenery, and enjoyed greatly the walks about the hills, and the charming landscapes, seldom surpassed, which abound in the vicinity of this village. I can recall his delight, too, in cloud scenery in the autumnal evenings, after we had passed our final examinations, and when we used to stroll together through field and forest. The sky scenery at night was also a source of joyous emotion, when it was sombre and solemn, especially— a type, I used to imagine, of his characteristic frame of mind.

One of my strongest impressions of my friend at the first, deepened by longer and intimate fellowship, was, what I may convey by the term "*noble.*" I could never associate May, in my mind (nor could any one who knew him even less intimately), with an act of meanness, anything low or vulgar. He had in him "the soul of honor," as my relations to him enabled me to verify in more ways than one. In one case, this was strikingly exemplified, the circumstances of which (known only to him and myself) have descended with him to the grave, but which I can recall as a silent tribute to his magnanimity.

Intellectually, May appeared to me then, in contrast with others and myself, to have *breadth;* a capacity for large views; a fondness for principles rather than details; a grasping after "the remoter relations," as one of our class-mates used to say; a prying into the mysterious, "obstinate questionings," as Wordsworth styles them. This peculiarity gave an additional charm to our mutual studies and discussions, and added to the strength of attachment in those who were among his more intimate college friends. This, too, greatly interested our preceptor (Dr.

Brown), and led him to anticipate much from his after career as a scholar. In the æsthetic portion of our curriculum he revelled with especial delight; and in the higher classics, taught by the President at that time, his exquisite taste was manifested and greatly developed. Since coming to this place, as President, I have frequent reminders of my friend, in the departments especially committed to me.

My friend's first religious impressions existed, no doubt, to some extent, before coming to college. I gathered this from our subsequent intercourse, which was in the highest degree confidential on all points. He and I occasionally attended the weekly prayer-meeting, conducted by the President, for the benefit of the students and villagers, on Thursday evenings, during the first winter after we came to college. Though always respectful, thoughtful, and eminently moral and conscientious, no distinctively spiritual feeling seemed to have been awakened in his heart, till the summer of 1823. In the early part of the summer session, several of the pious students, preparing for the ministry, became deeply concerned about their friends who were not Christians. They agreed among themselves to select, each one, a friend, for whom they resolved to pray, specially and earnestly, till they were brought unto the Kingdom. Among these, was *James May*. Neither he, nor any of us, was aware of this covenant. But prayer was answered by the awakening influence of the Holy Spirit, in his case and that of others. His convictions were deep and thorough " of sin and misery." He tarried longer in the valley of humiliation than many others, though probably the most upright and moral among the group of awakened

students. He had many doubts and great conflicts
of soul—was more like " Christian," in Bunyan's
Pilgrim's Progress, than " Hopeful." Even after he
was enabled to take hold of the Saviour, and gave
to others evidence of being truly converted, he
hesitated, and questioned the reality or thoroughness
of his change.   When he was examined and admitted to the communion, these doubts continued, and
he hesitated, and feared to make a profession of his
faith. After his first communion, the cloud was partially removed, but occasionally returned. After
seeming to enjoy great consolation in believing, " rejoicing in hope," and, as we all thought, finally
established in faith, he would again and again open
the question, and have " the spirit of bondage again
to fear." No one doubted his conversion, but himself. Dr. Brown thought it a radical and sound
case, and spoke of him with more assurance than of
others who had more emotional enjoyment. Quite
a large number of students were at that time brought
into the Church. Indeed, the religious interest pervaded almost the entire college ; a large proportion
being already professing Christians, who were thus
greatly improved in Christian graces and fitness for
usefulness. The season was always spoken of, and is
to this day, by the older people of the village and
vicinity, and by ministers, then either converted or
revived, as " the revival of 1823."

After leaving college, May and I corresponded for
some time. I am sorry, now, that on leaving my
recent place of pastoral labor, I destroyed those lovely
memorials of our friendship. During the rest of his
life, we met only twice, once on my way to Prince-
ton, in Pottsville, and again, casually, in Philadel-

phia. He did not finally determine on being a minister, till after he had made some progress in study for another profession. I watched with great interest his subsequent career as a Pastor, in the *lovely Valley of Wyoming;* as a Professor, in Virginia; as a firm advocate of Evangelical truth; as a martyr to his devotion to the cause of the nation; and then hoped, with the Church, for his usefulness in the sphere to which he was called in Philadelphia.

As I was not cognizant of his state of health, his death was to me a surprise, as well as grief. Of all

> " The friends so linked together,
> I've seen around me fall,"

since my college days here, no one is remembered so often and fondly as James May. While my relations and position have identified me with this place, I think he has never been in Canonsburg since we graduated together, September 25th, 1823. It was natural for me to anticipate, on my coming here, that he might be induced to come again to his Alma Mater, and that we might together talk of the days of " *long ago.*" You may fancy how rich and sweet would have been our mutual reminiscences of persons and events. With all his gravity, he had a keen sense of the ludicrous; and, like other colleges, ours furnished materials which now are forgotten by all but the actors. These he enjoyed at the time, and, no doubt, would have relished when recalled. But that now cannot be ; he is gone, with many others of my class. Instead of wandering with him, once more, over these hills, and recounting, here, the joys of other days, the companions of our studies, the mazes and mysteries of our different paths, I have only to anticipate the nobler and sweeter reunion above, on the everlasting hills.   Among the noble " spirits of the just made perfect," there is a solemn joy in the thought of meeting James May, as we used to say, in the language of John Foster, " in the sunlight of a brighter economy," " with a stormless sky, serenely calm forever."

APPENDIX.

LETTERS OF COMFORT TO A CHRISTIAN SUFFERER.

LETTER ON PRAYER-MEETINGS.

LETTER TO A YOUNG CHRISTIAN.

LETTER TO A CLERGYMAN.

LETTER ON ATTENDANCE AT CONVENTION.

11

LETTERS OF COMFORT.

THE letters which follow, to page 164, were addressed, by Dr. May, to a suffering friend in Philadelphia. They proved so great a comfort to him in his sickness, and contain in them so much of the appropriate Scriptural consolation for like cases, that it has been thought it would be a kindness to Christ's troubled ones, to put these words of cheer within their reach.

PHILADELPHIA, December 31, 1861.

MY DEAR FRIEND:

Religious duties call me out of the city every Saturday, and detain me till Monday. I shall not be able, in the interval, to see you in your chamber. I therefore substitute the pen for the tongue, in offering a few words of Christian and fraternal sympathy.

Your condition of suffering has been much in my mind since I saw you yesterday. I perceived, then, how great was your distress, amounting to anguish; and, though I spoke a word to comfort you, felt all the time how weak and inadequate was all that I could say. I would have the Lord speak to you. And may we not have some word to you from his mouth? Let us read what is written: "Shall we receive good at the Lord's hand, and shall we not receive evil?" So we read in Job. And then, in Isaiah, "I have chosen thee in the furnace of affliction." Observe, it is a "*furnace*" of affliction, to show its intensity. "For whom the Lord loveth, he chasteneth." And "no chastening, for the present, seemeth to be joyous, but grievous; nevertheless, afterward it yieldeth the peaceable fruit of righteousness to them that are exercised thereby." And, again, "What I do thou knowest not now; but thou shalt know hereafter."

You say you are a sinner before God. Most true, my dear friend; but "the blood of Jesus Christ cleanseth from all sin." "God made him who knew no sin to be sin for us, that we might be made the righteousness of God in him." What divinely spoken words! Christ takes our sins, bears them, and atones for them by his blood, and gives to us, through faith, his righteousness. Oh! that glorious righteousness, which is of God by faith! How it is fitted to the case, and adapted to all the wants of a sinful, condemned man! It is God's gift of grace. We are to stretch forth the hand to receive it, and it is ours. Now, does not the Lord seem to say to you, "Stretch forth *thy* hand,"—i. e., the hand of faith,—"and lay hold upon this righteousness?" It is a garment that will fully cover you; a pure, white raiment, in which you may be clothed, and no shame of any sinful nakedness appear.

My dear friend, I know man cannot comfort you. It is for God to do it. He tries your faith and patience for a time. But hold fast, hold fast to his word. Say to him, as Jacob said, "I will not let thee go, except thou bless me." Wrestle till break of day. You shall see the dawn, and have joy in the blessing. "All things are possible to him that believeth."

Truly, your friend,
JAMES MAY.

PHILADELPHIA, March 25, 1862.

MY DEAR FRIEND:

My very heart feels for you in your sufferings, and I earnestly pray for you and add an *Amen* to your own prayers for relief. The good Lord deals with you in wisdom; but he does not open to our minds the mystery of his dispensations. He leaves something for faith to trust him in. He calls on you to walk in the dark; but be assured of his presence. He allows the frail body to be an instrument of suffering; but the spirit within may be thereby disciplined, and prepared for the fulfilment of his hidden counsels. David could sing, "The Lord is my shepherd: I shall not want." "Though I walk through the valley of the shadow of death, I will fear no evil; for thou art with me: thy rod and thy staff, they comfort me." I believe the Lord is, in like manner, *your* Shepherd, though you may not perceive him. Job complained that he could not realize his presence, going backward or forward, on the right hand or on the left. And yet, added the afflicted patriarch, "He knoweth the way that I take: when he hath tried me, I shall come forth as gold."

You have "a merciful and faithful High Priest, who is touched with a feeling of your infirmities." He has been in all points tempted like as you are. He knows, consequently, how to feel for you. And when you hear his gracious invitation, "Come unto me, all ye that labor and are heavy laden, and I will give you rest," you may strengthen yourself in the Lord. Keep fast hold of this anchor, which entereth into that within the veil, and thereby have a "strong consolation."

I hope to see you very soon, and to hear from you good words of faith, and hope, and joy.

Very sincerely,
Your friend,
JAMES MAY.

PHILADELPHIA, April 3, 1862.

MY DEAR FRIEND:

If I had the power of Aaron or St. Paul, I would pronounce authoritatively the blessings of both the Old Testament and the New, and say, "The Lord bless thee and keep thee. The Lord make his face to shine upon thee and be gracious unto thee. The Lord lift up his countenance upon thee, and give thee peace;" and, also, "Grace, mercy, and peace, from God the Father and Jesus Christ our Lord." But, as I am neither Aaron nor St. Paul, I use the words as a prayer, that so it may be with you. I would it were the prayer of such strong faith as might bid the mountain of your sufferings be removed. If the mountain itself be not removed, we may hope for such help as shall lift you above it; that you may rise out of the mists of the valley, and look afar, even beyond the days of suffering, to the better country.

There is one who can effectually help you. I think he stands at the door, and knocks, ready to sup with you. He appeared to Daniel in the lions' den; to the three who were cast into the burning, fiery furnace; to Stephen, when stoned; to Peter, when in prison; to Paul, in the castle of Antonia; and to the great cloud of witnesses, who have, through much tribulation, entered into the Kingdom of God. He has laid a strong foundation for your soul's rest, the Rock of Ages. He has been under the curse; has suffered death, and tasted the bitter cup of anguish for your sins. And he is now in glory, with all power for the remission of sins. His blood,—his precious blood,—cleanseth from all sin. He is not simply a man in weakness, who cannot help. He is "the Son of God;" "the Lord of glory;" "God over all." He has the keys of death and hell. He opens, and no man can shut; he shuts, and none can open. Hear how majestically he speaks: "Fear not, thou worm Jacob: I will help thee, saith the Lord thy Redeemer, the Holy One of Israel." "I create the fruit of the lips: peace, peace to him that is far off, and to him that is near, saith the Lord; and I will heal him."

My own words are weak, and I give you the words of Jehovah. Jesus is Jehovah, our covenant God. Trust him fully. Venture on him for peace, hope, and joy. Yet remember that he does not always consent to our wishes as to the time for the bestowment of these gifts. When the sisters of Lazarus sent the message, "He whom thou lovest is sick," "he abode still two days in the same place," in seeming neglect of their affliction. But when he did go, it was in the full divinity of grace and power. "Your time," he said to his friends, on one occasion, "is always ready. My time is not yet full come." But his time did come. So shall it be in your case. Commit your way unto him, and he will bring it to pass. May he daily increase your faith; and may faith see his hands and his side, with assurance that he died for you, and now lives for you. May the joy of the Lord be your strength.

Truly, your friend,

JAMES MAY.

PHILADELPHIA, April 14, 1862.

MY DEAR FRIEND:

Be assured I do not forget you, either in Christian sympathy or prayer.   Your sufferings are very great, and it may seem to you, at times, that even the attentions and sympathy of friends avail but little for your relief and comfort.   They cannot relieve a body visited with such pains as yours, and may be able to do very little towards comforting a wearied mind.   May we not, however, point you to him who, having borne our sins and sicknesses, knows what they are, in even their greatest weight, and can feel *for* us and *with* us; and who, having overcome Satan and death, can minister relief with divine sufficiency.   You may say:

> " On him I lean, who, not in vain,
>   Experienced every human pain.
>   He feels my griefs ; he sees my fears;
>   And counts and treasures up my tears."

You know that he has said, " Only believe: all things are possible to him that believeth."   And though you complain often of weakness of faith, you can pray, " Lord, help mine unbelief."   That prayer was answered on a memorable occasion, and you may find an answer in your case.

Bodily sufferings we may not escape.   Nor can we always find a reason for them.   We must rest on the ground of simple faith; and, knowing that it is God's will that we should suffer, endeavor to glorify him in the fires.   The writer of the seventy-third Psalm was in most distressing perplexity, because of the sufferings of the servants of God, contrasted with the prosperity of the wicked.   So long as he tried to reason about the matter, and to satisfy his own understanding, he found no relief. It was not till he "*went into the sanctuary of God*," that his mind was brought to rest. In the sanctuary he looked at the whole matter from the stand of faith. Then he was ashamed of his former distrust and unbelief, and he exclaimed, " Whom have I in heaven but thee? And there is none upon earth that I desire besides thee! My flesh and my heart faileth; but God is the strength of my heart, and my portion forever."

The faithful under the Old Testament had to see things in a figure or shadow, or through a veil. And some of them failed to look through it to Christ, who is "the end of the Law for righteousness to every one that believeth." *We* now may see things clearly, because, the sun having arisen and gone up to the meridian, the shadows have been withdrawn, and, the veil having been torn from top to bottom at our Saviour's death, we can look in, yea, *enter* into the Holiest, and see Jesus lifted on the cross for our salvation, a full and perfect propitiation for our sins.

It is true that even the New Testament leaves much darkness on many things that we may wish to know. It does not explain why some are left to suffer such pains as you have suffered. But it does show that God chastens "for our profit, that we may be partakers of his holiness;" and that our afflictions are designed to " work out for us a far more exceeding and eternal weight of glory." And it opens to us a mighty Redeemer, who, after dying for our sins, is now seated in his glory, inviting our full faith as conqueror over sin, Satan, and death.

Behold, then, "this Lamb of God, that taketh away the sin of the world." Look unto Jesus, expiring on the cross, seated in glory, having all power in heaven and earth, "exalted to give repentance and remission of sins." You may know thus not only the power of his death, as an atonement for the sins of the world, but "the power of his resurrection." "The power of his resurrection!" Oh! what a power that is! It broke through the bonds of death, which had held all the dead from the time of Adam, and which would, but for the might of Christ's resurrection, have continued to hold them forever. "The power of his resurrection" gives life to faith. If you had to believe in one who died under the curse, and still remained in death, how could your faith have vigor? But you believe in one who says, "I am he that was dead and liveth, and behold I am alive forevermore, and have the keys of hell and death." Look, then, to him confidingly. Let your faith hold fast to a *living* Saviour—one living in all the fulness of God. "By death he has destroyed him that had the power of death, that is the Devil, and delivered them, who, through fear of death, were all their lifetime subject to bondage." Trust your body and soul to him, thus glorious and mighty, and, contemplating him in his resurrection, say, "O death, where is thy sting? O grave, where is thy victory?" "Thanks be to God who giveth us the victory through our Lord Jesus Christ." Amen, and Amen.

Truly, your affectionate friend,
JAMES MAY.

April 17, 1862.

My dear Friend:

I wish that I could be to you a bearer of glad tidings of peace and comfort. May I not be such, in the words of God's own sending? Has he not sent to you these words: "Peace I leave with you; my peace I give unto you?"

You need not fear. It is your privilege to go *boldly* to a throne of grace. "Open thy mouth wide," he says, "and I will fill it." He has taught us that "men ought always to pray, and not to faint." It may seem to you that your prayers are not heard. "But shall not God avenge his own elect, who cry day and night unto him? I tell you that he will avenge them speedily."

He requires our faith, even while we are led in a dark way. He leads the blind by a way that they know not: but it is that he may make darkness light before them, and crooked things straight. However deep may be the darkness, he is in the midst of it, and your faith may hear his call: "Fear not, for I am with thee: be not dismayed, for I am thy God." You know the Israelites were distressed at the Red Sea, the hosts of Pharaoh pursuing them behind, mountain heights on their right hand and on their left, and the sea before them. Yet how did the Lord show his presence in the pillar of cloud and fire; and how did he show the might of his hand in cutting them a way through the waters! He did not desert his people then, and can you think he will desert *you* now?

You say you are a sinner. Most true. Saul of Tarsus was, in his own estimate, "the chief" of sinners. And yet the Lord showed him great mercy, "for a pattern to all that should hereafter believe." The thief on the cross was a great sinner. Yet Jesus' blood cleansed him from all sin. Christ was "made *sin* for us"—a sin-offering. "He bore our sins in his own body on the tree." And who can put limits to the efficacy of that offering? " Though your sins be as scarlet, they shall be white as snow." " Where sin abounds, grace does much more abound." If Jesus were mere man, you might well fear to trust him ; for how can a mere man take away sins ? But he is " the Son of God," and has " all power in heaven and earth"—can save, therefore, " to the uttermost."

You say your faith is weak. But, though in measure as a grain of mustard seed, it may remove mountains. You can pray, "help mine unbelief." You have to do with not only a faithful, but a merciful High Priest, who will not break the " bruised reed, nor quench the smoking flax." " He will not contend forever, neither will he be always wroth." Look up, then, and lift up your head. Lift up your heart to the Lord. Lay hold of his covenant. Fall into his hands, for his mercies are great. " The name of the Lord is a strong tower :" you may run into it, and be safe. Be assured that Jesus, your Redeemer, has, " through death, destroyed him that had the power of death, that is the Devil; and delivers them, who, through fear of death, were all their lifetime subject to bondage." The sting of death he has received in himself, and so deprived it of its poison; and you may meet the last enemy as having no more power. He that believes in Jesus as his Saviour, "shall never taste of death." Trust him; and trust him to the last.

Truly, your affectionate friend,

JAMES MAY.

PHILADELPHIA, April 28, 1862.

MY DEAR FRIEND:

I feel deeply for you in your sufferings. To whom may we refer you for relief and comfort? Not to *man*. We are but flesh, and our flesh but dust. "We are crushed before the moth." But, "trust ye in *the Lord* forever, for in the Lord Jehovah is everlasting strength." Isaiah writes, "Why sayest thou, O Jacob, and speakest, O Israel, my way is hid from the Lord, and my judgment is passed over from my God? Hast thou not known, hast thou not heard, that the everlasting God, the Lord, the Creator of the ends of the earth, fainteth not, neither is weary?" "He giveth power to the faint, and to them that have no might, he increaseth strength. Even the youths shall faint and be weary, and the young men shall utterly fall. But they that wait upon the Lord shall renew their strength—shall run, and not be weary—shall walk, and not faint."

It is true, the Lord makes many of his promises to the Church, *as a body;* but they belong equally to *each member* of the body. We may appropriate them as though addressed to ourselves privately and particularly.

He promises to "lead the blind by a way that they knew not," and at the same time says, that he "will not forsake them." He has thus been leading you amidst the fires of suffering. But we believe

that if we could look into the furnace, we should see
with you, in its scorching heat, "one like unto the
Son of God." So, walking through the fire, you
shall not be burned. God knows how hot to make
the furnace, in order to effectually purify the gold;
and though he seem not to regard your cries and
tears, in the end you shall find, as Job did, that "the
Lord is very pitiful and of tender mercy." It
pleases him to keep his people in the dark awhile,
that the light may be the sweeter when he leads
them out of it.

You know how David complained, at times:
"Why art thou cast down, O my soul, and why art
thou disquieted within me?" and how he encouraged himself. "Hope thou in God, for I shall yet
praise him."

Do you ask, how long before the comfort comes
that you are waiting for? So did the Psalmist; for,
to sufferers, the time seems long. But, "with the
Lord, one day is as a thousand years, and a thousand
years as one day." Still, "he is not slack concerning his promises." "In due time we shall reap, if
we faint not." Do not distrust him. Take fast hold
of his promise, that he will not leave you comfort-
less, but will come to you. Touch the hem of his
garment, that virtue may come forth to heal your
soul. "He will not contend forever." "He con-
sidereth your frame, he remembereth that you are
dust." However dark may seem his ways, when he
leads you into suffering, "he seeth the end from the
beginning." Say, then, as Job did, when he was
dealt with as you are, "Though he slay me, yet will
I trust in him,"

" Judge not the Lord by feeble sense,
　　But trust him for his grace;
　Behind a frowning Providence
　　He hides a smiling face.
　His purposes will ripen fast,
　　Unfolding every hour;
　The bud may have a bitter taste,
　　But sweet will be the flower."

Your affectionate friend,
JAMES MAY.

PHILADELPHIA, May 3, 1862.

MY DEAR FRIEND:

I give you another token of remembrance. Accept it as a pledge of love in Christ. In Christ, I say, for are you not in him? Has he not redeemed you with a great ransom, the price of his own precious blood? Has he not called you to him as his child and friend? And whom he calls, he justifies; whom he justifies, he glorifies.

Look up, my friend, to Jesus. Though now in glory, he is not removed from faith. Look up; and though you may not see him, as St. Stephen did, your faith may lay hold on him as able to save you, even to the uttermost. Your soul may rest upon his precious promises. . . . . Trust him, trust him fully. He may often hide his face from you, but he will not withdraw from you his hand. He will not leave you nor forsake you.

A certain writer imagines that some of the animals in the ark with Noah were allowed to be in the very bottom of the vessel, where they had almost no light. And so some Christians, who are in the Church of God, may be in a deep hold, whence they cannot see the light coming from above, and may think that they are sinking in the dark waters. But if they are in the ark, they shall have a safe passage, though it be a sad and dreary one.   There is light, there is safety in the ark, though you may not see them or know whence they come.   God is not to be called by us to account.   He would have us " be still, and know that he is God."   " He chastens for our profit."   "And what son is he whom the father chasteneth not?"

Grace, mercy, and peace be multiplied unto you from God the Father and from Jesus Christ our Lord.

Your affectionate friend,
JAMES MAY.

May 10, 1862.

MY DEAR FRIEND:

I would hear *from* you a good word of faith and hope.   Can you not say, " I know whom I have believed, and am persuaded he is able to keep that which I have committed to him against that day?" I think there is a good word *for* you.   " *As many as I love*, I rebuke and chasten."

Let me repeat a remark I heard last evening from a friend to an acquaintance, who, in great distress of mind and body, was praying to be delivered : " Perhaps you are wrong in wishing to be relieved from trials, because the Lord, in his wisdom, may see that trials are best for you, and most wholesome.   You ought to pray rather for grace to bear the trials. Grace being received to enable you to bear them, the relief is found then in the inward strength imparted."   The remark seems to me to be just.   You know, when St. Paul had a thorn in the flesh, the messenger of Satan, sent to buffet him, he prayed thrice that it might be taken from him. His prayer, in one sense, was not granted, for the thorn was left still in the flesh. But, in another sense, it was replied to, for he received the assurance, " My grace is sufficient for thee." If I have a burden on my shoulders which is beyond my strength to bear, I may be relieved either by its being taken away, or by having a stronger than myself come in to bear it with me. Thus the Lord is ready to help *you*. " Cast thy burden on the Lord," says the Psalmist, " and he will sustain thee." If Jesus be with you in the waters, they shall not overflow you; and if with you in the fire, it shall not consume you. Better be chastened for our profit than to be without chastisement, and thus without proof of a father's love.

The Lord visits some of his children with more chastisement than others. Why, he does not explain. Abraham and Isaac seem, for the most part, to have led quiet and peaceable lives, while Job had bitter trials. The Infinitely Wise had his own purposes to serve, and does not allow us to know the secrets of his counsels. It is enough to know that love and mercy are at the bottom of them all. If not tried on our own account, we may be for the benefit of others, and for the glory of God. And, should he require you to walk in the dark, even such darkness that you may have to get down and feel your way, the end will show that he is wise, gracious, faithful, and full of love. Then you shall rise to praise him.

Affectionately, yours,
JAMES MAY.

May 10, 1862.

MY DEAR FRIEND:

When I left my letter at your door this morning, I hoped to be able to see you later in the day. Fearing that I may be disappointed, I write again to say that there is peace for you in Christ. He is himself our peace. He left a legacy of peace to us. " My peace I give (or bequeath) to you." I think he remembered you in that, his will. He remembers all for whom he died, and whom he calls to faith in him. And he has so called you. His words describe your case. " Come," he says, " all ye that labor and are heavy laden, and I will give you rest." Come to him, then, and trust in him. Look to him and live. Let him do as he will with you, and, in the conviction that he will make all work for good to you, say, " Not my will, but thine be done." "Let him do as seemeth to him good." Then, " though weeping endure for a night, joy cometh in the morning."

But I am giving you too much to read, and now only add an assurance of the affectionate remembrance of

Your sincere friend,
JAMES MAY.

May 15, 1862.

MY DEAR FRIEND:

I heartily wish I could give you a word effectual for your comfort, this morning. There are many, drawn from the Bible, which, in themselves, have all that is needful. Such are those sweet assurances, that "*whom the Lord loveth*, he correcteth,"—that " he chastens *for our profit*, that we may be partakers of his holiness,"—and that, although "no chastening for the present seemeth to be joyous, but grievous, nevertheless, *afterward*, it yieldeth the peaceable fruit of righteousness to them that are exercised thereby." I pray that you may find these so suited to your case, that they may suffice to instruct, strengthen, and comfort you.

God is leading you in a dark way, yet be assured he is himself not far off. His hand holds you; and if you listen, you may hear his voice, saying, "Fear thou not, for I am with thee; be not dismayed, for I am thy God."

You complain of sin. True, no man living can be justified in his sight; but his mercies are great, his loving-kindness infinite. Having given his Son for our redemption, shall he not, with him, also freely give us all things? Jesus, our Mediator, Surety, High Priest, and Lamb of God, answers for us, bears our sins, and takes them away. With them upon him, as our surety and propitiation, he died, and was laid down in the grave. But, though he carried them both to his death and burial, he did not bring them up again, when he arose. He left them in the grave, and went up in his glory. When he comes again, it will not be as a sin-bearer. For the Apostle says, "He shall appear the second time *without sin*, unto salvation." Sin having been atoned for and buried with himself, he will appear again, not as one humbled beneath the curse, but as one glorified for our salvation. You may look to him, therefore, not only as on the cross, bearing the agony and shame of your transgressions, but also as in glory, exalted to give repentance and remission of sins. So looking to him, you may have peace.

Be assured that he remembers you.   Some of his
followers sail on stormy seas, and seem to be driven
far from their course.   Others are ever borne on
smooth waters.   The same pilot directs both.   You
shall find that, in the darkest night and stormiest
waves, he is present, though unseen.   Trust him,
though you see him not.

Your affectionate friend,
JAMES MAY.

May 21, 1862.

MY DEAR FRIEND:

The longer I live, the more fully am I convinced
of the need of resting on the simple testimony of
the Bible.   God's word liveth and abideth forever.
It is quick and powerful.   It is the proper seed of
life.   We can rest our souls on no word as we may
on this.   And yet this blessed word has mysteries,
just as the course of Providence has mysteries, by
which our patience and our faith are tried.   "Secret
things belong to the Lord our God; things that are
revealed, to us and to our children."   He keeps it a
secret from us why some suffer, while others have
enjoyments; and why he does not answer prayer at
the time and in the manner we desire.   But some
things are made clear enough.   Among these are,
our duty to hold fast by his word; to walk with him,
even though in the dark; and to be still, and know
that he is God.   Sometimes our will may be un-
yielding.   Then he may find it needful to press the
yoke on us more heavily.   We may not understand
it, for he is a God that hideth himself, and does not
allow his purpose to be known till the end comes.
"What I do," said our Saviour to Peter, "thou

knowest not now; but thou shalt know hereafter."
Abraham did not know the meaning of the command to offer Isaac for a burnt-offering, till the conclusion of the matter showed it. Jacob did not
know the meaning of his beloved Joseph being lost
to him, till more than twenty years had passed,
when it was made plain. Job could not explain the
mystery of his sufferings, till the issue made all
clear. You may find as much darkness in your
case as either of those mentioned, but it is no chance
which has happened to you. Our heavenly Father
does not let a sparrow fall to the ground without
him, and the very hairs of our heads are all num-
bered. Still, he does not permit us to question him
as to the reasons for his dealings with us. He requires faith and patience,—faith in his kind purposes; patience to wait for their development. To
one of the sisters of Lazarus, who seemed almost
ready to complain because he did not come as soon
as sent for, he answered, " Said I not unto thee, that
if thou wouldst believe, thou shouldst see the glory
of God?" While to his mother, at the wedding
feast in Cana, and to his brethren, urging him to do
at once what they desired, he said, " My time is not
yet come."

His time for giving you relief is not yet fully come,
he seems to say. " Wait on the Lord," is now the
lesson. Trust him for all that is to be. When all
fails but himself, he will appear. He did not stay
Abraham's hand till Isaac was bound on the wood,
and the knife uplifted for the sacrifice. You may
ever pray, " Increase my faith," and also ask for
grace to bear what he puts on you, having assurance
that, in the end, you shall " see the glory of God."

He who bore your sins, who was made a curse for you, and offered his blood as an atonement, will not, now that he lives for evermore in glory, leave you to the enemy.   Lift up your heart to him, and trust him fully.   That you may do so, prays

Your affectionate friend,

JAMES MAY.

BALTIMORE, May 26, 1862.

MY DEAR FRIEND:

I trust that if you are still walking in the valley of Baca, you find in it a well.   It is true that there are vast and dreary deserts on earth, and travellers do at times find themselves in the midst of them, without water.   But you remember that when the children of Israel were distressed from such a cause, God, their God, showed himself able to provide. Moses was commanded to smite the rock, and water flowed from it abundantly.   In the dry desert of this world, a like refreshment is provided for yourself. The spiritual Rock that has been smitten for you, and for all poor travellers upon the way to Canaan, pours forth its streams for you, and you are called to drink.   Love, mercy, grace, flow freely from the great fountain in Christ Jesus.   And it is not a hidden fountain.   You do not have to look for Christ in heights above, or in the depths beneath.   He is present to you by his word and Spirit; and he is strong enough to save you.   He is true and faithful to his promises to save.   He is full of love and of compassion, willing and free to save.

> "All the fitness he requireth,
> Is to feel your need of him."

I had occasion, yesterday, to preach here (in Baltimore), from the text, "Behold, I lay in Zion a chief corner-stone, elect, precious: and he that believeth on him shall not be confounded." That corner stone is Jesus, and you may be assured of its sufficiency to bear you up. To some, indeed, it becomes a stone of stumbling, because they know not its qualities nor its proper place. But you know where to put Christ in your faith, that is, at the foundation. All hope is to be built on him, all trust to repose on him. He can abundantly sustain. In him you have redemption, and in him salvation, full and sure. He who pardoned the thief dying on the cross, can pardon you. You may pray, "Lord, remember me, now thou art in thy kingdom," and he will hearken, and deliver you.

Your affectionate friend,

JAMES MAY.

PHILADELPHIA, May 31, 1862.

MY DEAR FRIEND:

"Grace, mercy, and peace from God the Father and the Lord Jesus Christ!" You have heard and read of the exceeding grace of God to the chief of sinners, and have been disposed to ask, is such grace for *you?* Yes, it abounds to you, as to all that are called into the fellowship of Jesus Christ. And are you not called? The table of the Gospel feast is large; all things are ready; and the servants are sent out to proclaim the fact. If you do not think yourself one of the first called, perhaps you may be willing to be classed among the poor, the maimed, the halt, and blind, that were to be compelled to come in. Is not the Lord using compulsion with you? Is he not pressing the call most urgently; laying a heavy hand upon you; and, as in the case of Lot, impelling you to go where he desires? Thus powerfully are you called and pressed to come; the feast provided for you is abundant; and there is room, and a wedding garment for you, too. You cannot linger. You must yield, and take your seat with the rejoicing guests at the marriage supper of the Lamb. "O thou of little faith, wherefore dost thou doubt?" Jesus himself calls. He is himself present. You are not ignorant of his person, of his power, or of his grace. Exceeding riches of grace they are. What a price is his blood paid for your redemption. Is it not enough to ransom you, and millions like you? No matter how many, nor how great, your sins, " Come," he says, " come unto me, and I will give you rest."

It may not please God to take away your sufferings yet. You may need a little more of the furnace-fire to purify the gold. But you can pray for faith, patience, and strength to bear. God allows us to seek such graces. So let us pray and trust. To all your prayers for such blessed fruits, I will say, Amen and Amen.

Your affectionate friend,

JAMES MAY.

PHILADELPHIA, June 5, 1862.

MY DEAR FRIEND:

My writing you a few lines, as you request, from time to time, is a very small contribution to the means of relieving your wearisome hours. I gladly undertake it, if it can give any variety to your daily routine of sorrowful thoughts. " To write is" (I may say) "to me not grievous." I would that I could add, with St. Paul, " but for you it is safe." It must always be safe, if we use the topics which the Scriptures give. There are two grand subjects they present in contrast with each other: our own emptiness, and the fulness of our Lord. On one side is sin, on the other side is righteousness; on one side weakness, on the other power. Can there be a transfer? Does not St. Paul say (2 Cor. 5 : 21), "He hath made him to be sin for us, that we might be made the righteousness of God in him?" Our sins are put to his account, he being our surety; and his righteousness is put to our account, as though we, in him, had fulfilled the law. "He has redeemed us from the curse of the law, being made a curse for us." This grand truth of the Bible, that Christ bore our sins, may well be seized and held fast by our faith. He is able both to bear and answer for them. And in his agony in Gethsemane, in his death upon the cross, we see what it cost to bear them. Well may the Apostle argue: "If, when we were enemies, we were reconciled to God by the death of his Son, much more, being reconciled, we shall be saved by his life." "He ever liveth to make intercession for us." And in the power of the endless life which he has in glory, he cannot be defeated. He has begun to reign, and his enemies are falling under his feet. The last enemy to be destroyed is death. From this last enemy he has already taken the sting, which is sin, and will eventually take away even the power over our poor bodies. For though death may turn them to dust, and seem to have the mastery, the power thus exercised will be destroyed at the resurrection. What can we ask more?

Your affectionate friend,

JAMES MAY.

PHILADELPHIA, June 12, 1862.

MY DEAR FRIEND:

The Master, when he sent forth his servants to their work, said, " When ye enter into a house, say, ' Peace be to this house.' " He assured them that if the Son of Peace were there, their peace should rest upon the household. Is there not to *you* a message of peace ? In the legacy of the same Master he says, " My peace I give unto you; not as the world giveth, give I unto you." The world would give peace, in the sense of quiet as to all outward discomforts and distresses. No so the Divine Master. He bestows his gifts, often the most precious, in the midst of painful sufferings. He chooses his people " in the furnace of affliction." Did he not so deal with Israel in Egypt, with Job, and with the long line of the faithful, who, before they " died in faith," " were destitute, afflicted, tormented ?"

In all such things the Lord does according to his own good pleasure. Some seem born to suffer; others, to have a peaceful pilgrimage to the promised land. In all cases, however, wisdom and mercy rule. The highest good of each individual is aimed at, and all will see cause to praise and bless God in the end.

You have been put on the rack, and made to pass through the fire. But look and see what God has done for you. Has he not led you thus far safely through the wilderness ? Has he not borne you as on eagles' wings ? Has he not sent his word and Spirit, to call you to the knowledge of himself? Has he not made himself known to you as your Redeemer, a covenant God, the Mighty One of Jacob ? Has not his grace abounded to you? In your sufferings, he has seemed to say, "What I do, thou knowest not now; but thou shalt know hereafter." We must be content to know that "he doth not willingly afflict, nor grieve the children of men." "He chastens for our profit."

It would be *pleasant* always to see his face shining on us; but it might not be *profitable.* A ceaseless sunshine would parch the soil, and destroy all hope of fruit. There must be clouds and storms, and sometimes floods. The Son of God himself was "made perfect through sufferings." On the cross he cried, "My God, my God, why hast thou forsaken me?" Our God calls you to trust him; to trust even in the dark, and when his face is turned away from you. Do your sins discourage you, and make you fear? The Redeemer has himself borne them, and made full satisfaction for them by shedding his own precious blood. That satisfaction has been proved sufficient by its being accepted of the Father, who has raised Christ from the dead, and set him at his own right hand in heaven. You may, then, fully rely on it. You may go to Christ's blood, day by day, and wash, and be clean. You may look up to him now in glory, and ask for the descent of the Spirit into your heart, to be to you a spirit of adoption, whereby you may cry, "Abba, Father." So may it ever be.

I conclude as I began, "Peace be to your house."

Your affectionate friend,

JAMES MAY.

June 17, 1862.

MY DEAR FRIEND:

I have occasion to be absent from the city to-day, and may not be able to see you as usual. I write to assure you that I do not forget you. But *my* remembrance of you is a small matter. *God* does not forget you. He may seem to overlook your sorrows, but he has riches of goodness and love, and dispenses them freely, though not according to our rule. He sees through all time, and understands what is best for us with reference to the distant future, as well as the present hour.

To the child, the discipline of a restraining or correcting parent may appear severe. But the parent, looking beyond the present pleasure of the child, does, in this exercise of discipline, what is best for the whole life and character. In after years, the child himself will testify to the wisdom and true kindness of the parent's course. You may remember what is written: "No chastening for the present seemeth to be joyous, but grievous; nevertheless, afterward it yieldeth the peaceable fruit of righteousness."

The Lord "doth not willingly afflict." Our good is aimed at always. Our prayers are answered, too, though sometimes it is "by terrible things in righteousness." But his mercy is not far off. How sweetly and how frequently does David sing, "His mercy endureth forever." He requires of us confidence in that mercy. "Only believe," is his voice to us. The lesson of faith began to be learned at the gate of Paradise; for it was "by faith" that "Abel offered unto God a more acceptable sacrifice than Cain." The long line of the faithful, from that

point onward, who make up the " great cloud of
witnesses," did not live to " see the promises" (*i. e.*,
the blessings promised), but "were persuaded of
them, and embraced them." *We* see their fulfilment, for the promised one has come. The good
things formerly just shadowed forth, we have in substance. " We are come . . . . to the blood of
sprinkling, which speaketh better things than that
of Abel." To the promises of mercy and redemption, thus fulfilled in Jesus, I commend you. May
you be persuaded of them, and embrace them, and
go onward in the strength and comfort of them in
your pilgrimage. If you think you, in your weakness, need a staff, take the Divine assurance, " My
grace is sufficient for thee." Lean on it; and in following on to know the Lord, you shall be upheld,
and find that " he is merciful and gracious," and
that " his compassions fail not." Our prayers are
for your peace and joy in God.

Your affectionate friend,

JAMES MAY.

PHILADELPHIA, June 25, 1862.

MY DEAR FRIEND :

If to comfort you depended on resources in myself
I should have no use for my pen, for none but the
All-sufficient can avail for your peculiar need. And
hear him say, " Come unto me, all ye that labor and
are heavy laden, and I will give you rest." This is
the language of divine fulness, for who but one that
has infinite perfections can give assurance from himself of rest to *all* that suffer ? There are those whose
trials no mere human power can relieve. But
Jesus excepts none from the class to whom he offers

rest. He heals the broken heart, binds up the wounded spirit, casts out evil spirits, commands the winds and the sea, "and they obey him." To him I must commend you.

I know, you sometimes think your prayers, and those of others for you, are not heard. But remember the words of the Prophet, "Why sayest thou, O Jacob, and speakest, O Israel, my way is hid from the Lord, and my judgment is passed over from my God? Hast thou not known, hast thou not heard, that the everlasting God, the Lord, the Creator of the ends of the earth, fainteth not, neither is weary? There is no searching of his understanding." His unsearchable understanding takes a view of things which we cannot. He sees the end from the beginning. We see the present process only, and are in distress. Job suffered long, and knew not why. He longed for the grave as the only place of rest. But when the end came, and the curtain was lifted, so as to reveal what was behind, the reason for his trials was made evident. And we can now see in his case that the Lord is wise and good in all his ways, as well as "pitiful and of tender mercy."

When one is shut up in the dark, the world may all seem dreary to him, however splendidly the sun be shining in the outer sky. *Your* horizon, now that you are in a gloomy valley (or, as you think, a pit), may seem narrow, dark, and fearful. But, could you rise to the hill-top near you, and look off to the distant lines beyond, you might see light and cheerful prospects, and all that can give hope and comfort. Faith may do this. And, though your faith may be but feeble now, yet I am sure that, on your midnight sky, stars may be seen. Can you not look up, and see, and sing of, at least one, as Kirke White did, when he wrote:

> "Once on the raging seas I rode;
> The storm was loud, the night was dark;
> The ocean yawned, and rudely blowed
> The wind that tossed my found'ring bark.
> Deep horror then my vitals froze;
> Death-struck, I ceased the tide to stem;
> When, suddenly, a star arose,—
> It was the star of Bethlehem.
> It was my guide, my light, my all;
> It bade my dark forebodings cease;
> And through the storm and danger's thrall,
> It led me to the port of peace."

That, in the language of the last verse, you may sing,

> "Now safely moored, my perils o'er,
> I'll sing first in night's diadem,
> Forever and forever more,
> The star, the star of Bethlehem,"

is the sincere prayer of your affectionate friend,

JAMES MAY.

PHILADELPHIA, June 30, 1862.

MY DEAR FRIEND:

Vacation having come, I am about to visit a brother in the country, and shall not return to the city till next week.

I am truly sorry to miss my visits to you for so long. But you shall not be forgotten in sympathy and prayer. Better than all, *God* does not forget you.

Look at "the Silent Comforter" hanging in your chamber. Read therein words spoken as never man spake. Read of Faith's victory. Faith overcomes not only the world, but death, and shouts the triumph, "O Death, where is thy sting? O Grave, where is thy victory?"

Death may have pains, but has no sting or poison to those who are in Christ. The surgeon's knife may cause great suffering, but is meant to cure, not to destroy. And death, though it involve much anguish to the Christian, relieves, by its sharp surgery, all earthly ills, and introduces to a perfect ease.

You know what takes away the sting of death, the blood of Jesus, which, taking sin away, deprives death of its power to ruin us. The posture of the sinner desirous to be saved is that of the Israelite in the wilderness, who, when he was bitten by a fiery serpent, looked to the serpent God caused to be lifted up, and thus lived. So may you look to Christ, and live. He says, "I am the Resurrection and the Life;" and, "As Moses lifted up the serpent in the wilderness, even so must the Son of Man be lifted up, that whosoever believeth in him should not perish, but have eternal life."

To him and to his saving grace I now commend you. Believe and live.

Your affectionate friend,
JAMES MAY.

WARWICK FURNACE, July 3, 1862.

MY DEAR FRIEND:

I must give you a pledge of remembrance, now that I am beyond the lines of a visit to you.

I do trust you have a recess from your sufferings. You find a mystery in their measure both of severity and continuance. You often ask, when will your Heavenly Father hear your call, and give you relief. " It is not for us to know the times or the seasons which God hath put in his own power." " His judgments are a great deep." We cannot fathom them. They are beyond our power of finding out, partly because, for a trial of our faith, they are purposely kept out of reach, and partly because, from the nature of them, their absolute depth, they are unfathomable. No human mind can sound them. We are too short-sighted to see into the depths of the great profound beneath, or to the amplitudes of the vast space above us. " God is in heaven, and we upon earth." " His thoughts are not as our thoughts, nor his ways as our ways." But we may confide in his wisdom, pity, grace, and love.

His grace ! how full the riches of it ! How has it abounded, and does yet abound to you ! You have been led as the blind, by a way that you know not. God has visited you, both in love and chastisement. The latter, St. Paul shows, is one proof of the former. It is the evidence of a wise, paternal care. " Whom the Lord loveth, he chasteneth, even as a father the son in whom he delighteth." If we be without chastisement, whereof all God's true children are partakers, we lack one testimony of our being really his children. Your sufferings are intended as a medicine, a surgical remedy, the cure from which will, in the end, repay you for the pain.

Keep your eye on him who was lifted up for the life of the world. Look to him in the divine excellency of his person, and the riches of his grace, especially as these are demonstrated in his sufferings. Think of him as loving you till death, and dying that your soul might live. And take hold of his blessed word of promise, " Him that cometh unto

me, I will in no wise cast out." Our place is at his
feet, but he permits us to look to him. "Only believe : all things are possible to him that believeth."

Your affectionate friend,

JAMES MAY.

PERKIOMEN, July 25, 1862.

MY DEAR FRIEND :

The Lord purposes that our whole term on earth
shall be a course of discipline and probation. In
such a course, we must expect, not enjoyments simply, but also trials, sometimes bitter ones. Without these, there could not be probation. We are
apt to look on life, especially in early years, as given
for enjoyment. We try to make our mountain strong.
We surround ourselves with friends and comforts.
But how easily can God overthrow our strongest
foundations ! He means that we shall not trust in
what we establish for ourselves. He would draw
our trust away from all that comes between himself
and us. He would make us see and own that he is
our refuge and strength. The lesson may be a hard
one for us, but we must learn it. And we learn
best in the school of experience, perhaps a painful
experience, too. But the pain shall not continue
always. "Heaviness may endure for a night, but
joy cometh in the morning." We may sow in tears,
but it is to reap in joy. Medicine may be bitter,
but cure and health come from it. I have no
doubt that the Lord, who is dealing with you through
bitter trials, has in store a blessing of peace and joy.
His grand purposes reach across ages—how much
more across the few years of life. It is not your
comfort for one or two years that he has regard to,

but your sanctification through the whole endless being of the soul.

The child may think the confinement and discipline of school to be nothing but a hard and useless appointment. But the father looks far into future years, and constrains the child in its first days, in order that mature life may have the advantage. The grand lesson to be learned is faith in God's wise ordering. If we can say, "It is the Lord, let him do what seemeth him good," then all is well. Then God comes nigh to us. We see his glory in the face of Jesus Christ. We perceive that his purposes are full of love. And, trusting in him, we have peace. So may it be with you.

Your affectionate friend,
JAMES MAY.

PHILADELPHIA, September 18, 1862.

MY DEAR FRIEND:

Let me remind you that the Lord, not man, is directing your steps. You would not have chosen the wearisome, dark road through which you have been led by his wise providence. He, for the accomplishment of his own purposes of love and goodness, has chosen it for you. "Affliction cometh not forth of the dust; neither doth trouble spring out of the ground."

Again, be reminded, that when God sends suffering, he always sends some alleviating circumstances. "He stayeth his rough wind in the day of the east wind." An apostle says, "He will not suffer us to be tempted above what we are able to bear." He will either temper for us the hot furnace, or give us patience to endure it.

Still further, let me recall his promise: " My grace is sufficient for thee." If you do not realize that sufficiency at present, you may pray for strength that is fully according to your day, and it will not be withheld. God may delay his answer, or answer only with what seem to you *crumbs* of favor. But be sure of his promises. Take fast hold of them. Be as Israel, who would not let the heavenly wrestler go, till a blessing was made sure to him. Trust God in all circumstances. Trust him to the end.

Shall Satan be able to say, " Here was a man who rested on God's promises, and yet was cast off without mercy ?" No, verily. " He that believeth shall not be confounded." God will give the adversary no such advantage. He is jealous for the honor of his word and character, and you shall find in him no failure. Remember, he has made a covenant with his people, and confirmed it by an oath, " that by two immutable things (the promise and the oath) by which it is impossible for God to lie, we might have strong consolation," in the double certification of his faithfulness. Such assurance may be an anchor to your soul sure and steadfast. It may keep you safe, both on the stormy sea of life, and amidst the beating of the cold, dark waves of death.

Your affectionate friend,
JAMES MAY.

PHILADELPHIA, October 7, 1862.

MY DEAR FRIEND :

There are good things enough in the word of God to fill our memories and feed our souls till life shall end. What better than God's covenant, as he made it with Abraham, and through him, as father

of the faithful, with all believers to the end of time?
With the Patriarch it seemed to secure only tempo-
ral good, such as possession of the land of Canaan
for his descendants. But our Saviour teaches us
what is implied in Jehovah's declaring himself " the
God of Abraham, of Isaac, and of Jacob:" " He is
not the God of the dead, but of the living." When
he made himself known to Moses thus, the patri-
archs had been dead more than two hundred years;
and yet he spoke of them as yet living; living not
on earth, but in the city for which they had been
looking, the city that hath foundations.

What is implied in his being the God of Jacob,
we see in Jacob's history. He led the Patriarch
through life; ordered his steps; guided and watched
over him; protected him in danger, angels ascend-
ing and descending to guard his way; and, though
he left him in perplexity and doubt for more than
twenty years over his lost Joseph, he yet, at last,
showed him the same Joseph alive, and ruler over all
the land of Egypt,—the preserver of himself and all
his house from perishing by famine.

That is a faint illustration of what God is to those
with whom he has made his covenant. The covenant embraces all things that are provided in Christ
for those whom he has redeemed. Has he not taken
you within the fold of that covenant? Has he not
redeemed you, called you to faith in himself, led
you, chastened you, and showed that he treats you
as a son? Has he not lifted the light of his countenance upon you, and at times, at least, given you
his peace? And will he now leave you? No. He
says, " I will never leave thee, nor forsake thee."
Nothing can separate you from the love of God

14

which is in Christ Jesus, our Lord.   Weak faith he
reproves, but does not despise.   " The bruised reed
he shall not break."   At the very time when he re-
buked Peter, sinking in the waves, for his slight
faith in him, he stretched forth a mighty hand to
hold him up.   And if your faith be weak, he will
not cast you out.   He may reprove; but oh ! how
graciously he teaches, trains, and nourishes you !
You may not see his hand, nor hear his voice, yet
he is near to bless.   Who saw him, when he guided
Joseph's steps, from the time he left his father's
house till he became governor over all the land of
Egypt?   Yet, when his plans were perfected, his
guidance of his servant was made clear.   Though
you see him not, and may appear to be in darkness,
he is guiding you.   He would have you trust that
guidance, and feel that all your times are in his
hand.   His judgments may be a great deep, but his
loving-kindnesses are infinite.   Trust him at all times,
then.   Be strong in faith, giving glory to God.

Your affectionate friend,

JAMES MAY.

PHILADELPHIA, October 14, 1862.

MY DEAR FRIEND :

Luther, it is said, used to remark that he was not
satisfied with an absolute God,—one whom he must
speak of simply as *God*,—but wanted one of whom
he could say, *My* God !—*i. e.*, one in whom he had
an interest, and who demonstrated an interest in
him.   The God of the Bible reveals himself as the
God of his redeemed people, saying, " They shall be
my people, and I will be *their God*."   He has a pro-
perty in them, and they in him.   He revealed him-

self to Moses under the incommunicable name "I Am," or "Jehovah;" but at the same time added, "I am the God of Abraham, the God of Isaac, and the God of Jacob; this is my name forever, and this is my memorial, throughout all generations."

This relationship, of being *the God of his people*, grows out of his covenant, in which, while he chooses and calls them to be his own, he pledges himself for their redemption, and promises such good things as could not have been otherwise conceived. He becomes their daily guide and preserver; supplies them with his grace, comprehending all the gifts of the Holy Spirit; and then, in the end, becomes their portion and everlasting possession. What he wants from them, meanwhile, is simple trust in him—trust, even when he hides his counsels in deep darkness. How dark his purpose, when he commanded Abraham to offer Isaac for a burnt offering! No explanation was given, yet Abraham was to trust his God, to do his bidding, and wait the development of his design. To *you*, no explanation is given why you suffer; yet you are to acquiesce in the Divine will, with the assurance that it is right, and that God means it for your good. The discipline may be hard and sore, but his good hand is in it. And you may fully trust him with the disposal of yourself. He did not fail Abraham : he will not fail you.

Your affectionate friend,
JAMES MAY.

PHILADELPHIA, October 21, 1862.

MY DEAR FRIEND:

You have observed, in the Epistle to the Hebrews, how the sacred writer puts forward the divine Redeemer. He calls attention both to his *rank*, as Son of God, and to his *office*, as High Priest for man.

In the former, he is above Moses, above angels, above all created things. In the latter, " it behooved him to be made like unto his brethren." As Son of God he prepared for us a great salvation; offered himself, through the Eternal Spirit, without spot, unto the Father; secured, thus, full propitiation for our sins; and now " ever liveth, to make intercession for us." As Son of man, he was " made perfect through sufferings," and gives us every reason to believe that he is " a High Priest who can be touched with the feeling of our infirmities." He is not separated from us by such a difference of nature and of rank as allows nothing in common between him and us. He is one with us in nature, in infirmity, in trials,* and in suffering, and so can feel with us. His sympathy is true, deep, and abiding.

Come boldly, my dear friend, to this divine yet human Saviour. There is nothing to keep you at a distance. Coming to him, you may be sure of power to help and save; for he has all power in heaven and in earth. You may be sure of a sacrifice of expiation; for " by one offering he has perfected forever them that are sanctified." You may be sure of grace; for he encourages you to come and find grace to help you in your time of need. You may be sure of sympathy; for he has had trial of infirmities and sufferings, and thus knows how to feel for us. And you may be sure of never-failing advocacy of your cause; for he abideth a priest continually, living to plead for us at the mercy-seat.

---

* Of course, excepting such as come from inward sin.

Consider, then, this Apostle and High Priest of our profession. Rely on him confidingly, and run with patience the race set before you, looking unto Jesus. He then will be with you to the end. He will not leave you.

Your affectionate friend,

JAMES MAY.

PHILADELPHIA, November 4, 1862.

MY DEAR FRIEND:

Though to you there may seem to be no speed in God's interposition for your relief, "the Lord is not slack concerning his promise, as some men count slackness." It is well that "the times and seasons" are not in our power. We should make but sad work, if we should be allowed to say when his word is to be fulfilled. Better to leave all in God's hands. He takes his time for it; but he delivers gloriously. See how he made Job's sorrows end, and how he brought to a glorious issue the troubles of Jacob, who had said that he should go down to the grave to his son mourning. "Our light afflictions, which are but for a moment," says St. Paul, "work out for us a far more exceeding and eternal weight of glory." Then, may they not be borne? You feel the burden of them greatly; but God is able to make you stand.

In yourself, you may feel very weak. The more you feel this, the better; for then you may be "strong in the Lord and in the power of his might." His strength, you know, is made perfect in weakness. Rest, then, in the arms of God, your strength and your Redeemer. Apart from him, you can have no safety. In him, you are in a strong tower. Be willing to walk in any darkness where he leads. He is not one that will forsake you. He extends the hand of power and mercy for your guidance and support. Trust him, then, even when you cannot see; for we must walk by faith, not by sight. His presence and his mighty arm are ever at hand.

Your affectionate friend,

JAMES MAY.

PHILADELPHIA, November 11, 1862.

MY DEAR FRIEND:

"If any man sin,"—such is the testimony of an apostle,—"we have an Advocate with the Father." Read the words with emphasis: "*If any man sin.*" If *you* sin, and feel your sin a burden, *you* have an Advocate with the Father, not a merely human friend, but "Jesus Christ the righteous." He is the Son of God, the all-sufficient Intercessor, divine as well as human in his nature, and fully commissioned to do for you all that your case needs. You may rely on him with full trust of soul. If you see your sins as a great debt, which you can never pay, remember that he, as surety, and as the propitiation for your sins, has made payment with his blood, and the payment is complete.

Remember, too, he is not merely one who lived on earth so many years ago, and then died, and was buried. He liveth now, yea, *ever liveth*, to make intercession for us. And he does not live merely in the heavens. He says to his disciples, "I will come to you, and make my abode with you." He is present with you by his Spirit; and that in power, in love, and grace. Turn your mind towards him. Let your faith take hold of him. By faith hold fast to him, as the Lamb of God that taketh away the sins of the world. He will be to you not only a propitiation, but a comforter; comforter, because propitiation,—a present help in time of need. He will not leave you nor forsake you, and will give you victory over sin and death.

Your affectionate friend,
JAMES MAY.

PHILADELPHIA, November 25, 1862.

MY DEAR FRIEND:

God's ways are not as our ways, nor his thoughts as our thoughts. It pleases him to afflict and chasten even those who most faithfully serve him. *Why*, in particular cases, we cannot see. We may know only, in a general way, that he means it for good, and that he makes all "work for good" to those that love him. We must be content with his word here, and leave it to him to unfold his purposes in his own time. *We may need discipline ourselves;* and it may come to wean us from the world, to bring us nearer to our Saviour, and to make us long for heaven; *and if we do not need it for ourselves, God may impose it on us for the benefit of others.* Paul suffered much for the advantage of the Churches which he founded. And he suffered for his own advantage also; for even *he* needed a thorn in the flesh, the messenger of Satan, to buffet him, lest he should be exalted above measure. It may be that extraordinary marks of the divine regard need extraordinary means of personal humiliation. The clear sun, at its meridian, would dazzle us, were not a shade or colored glass interposed between it and the eye. Affliction may be the needed shade between us and the otherwise blinding brightness of God's favor. It teaches us our weakness; makes us often conscious of much sin; and thus helps to keep us in a proper posture of humility.

There may be mystery in it; but God will make all plain hereafter. If we could clear up every obscurity and difficulty now, there would be no room for trustful confidence in God. We should, in such case, walk by reason, by understanding, or by sight, and not by faith. We must be schooled to trust God as Abraham trusted him, when, at his call, he went out, not knowing whither he went. You are now being subjected to this schooling. You go forward in the dark, not aware whither your sufferings tend, nor what shall be the measure or the end of them. You are to walk by faith here. Keep fast hold of the promises. Though you see not the Divine presence, you may hear the voice that says, "Follow me:" "Have faith in God." "All things are possible to him that believeth." Ever look unto Jesus, with readiness to bear the cross and follow him.

Your affectionate friend,
JAMES MAY.

PHILADELPHIA, December 3, 1862.

MY DEAR FRIEND:

I pray daily that you may have peace in mind and rest in body, and trust I may hear that the Lord gives you both. He does not, however, always see fit to do so. David had sometimes to call to him out of the depths. He speaks of being laid in darkness, in the deep, as though in spirit he had to go down to the grave. But his sorrows had their relief, though not in every case at once. He had to wait and hope for light. Sometimes it came in glimpses, and then went out, and left him in the dark again; so that he seemed to be sinking down below all light, and trust, and hope. Still, he was not forsaken. "Whom have I in heaven but thee," he says to God, "and there is none upon earth that I desire besides thee. My flesh and my heart faileth, but God is the strength of my heart, and my portion forever." "Why art thou cast down, O my soul? and why art thou disquieted within me? hope thou in God: for I shall yet praise him, who is the health of my countenance, and my God."

Now, may I not call on you to gird yourself, stand, and make answer? Wherefore dost *thou* doubt? Who art thou, that thou shouldest be afraid of evils which God, thy God, hath put beneath thy feet? Dost thou tremble at the darkness of the valley where the last great conflict must take place? Is not thy God there with his rod and staff to guide, protect, and comfort thee? Dost thou not know his loving kindness, yea, "the multitude of his mercies?" Is it said, you are a sinner? Be it so. If you were not such, you would need no Saviour and no mercy. The Gospel would not be for you, for its glad tidings is that "Jesus Christ came into the world *to save sinners.*" Now, let me call on you, poor sinner as you are, down in the lower depths of darkness, lift up your eyes, and see the light that is already shining down into your pit of suffering. It may seem only starlight, but it is the light of the bright and morning star, the herald of the day. Look up, and see it. "It is the star, the star of Bethlehem;" your guide to Jesus, and the comfort that there is in him. Arise and follow, and the Lord shall put a new song into your mouth, even praise to our God; for he that followeth Jesus shall not walk in darkness, but shall have the light of life.

Your affectionate friend,

JAMES MAY.

PHILADELPHIA, December 12, 1862.

MY DEAR FRIEND:

I am unable to pay you my usual visit, to-day. But if the Lord be with you, man's company and help may well be spared. I trust that he is ever with you. You know that he was with the lonely Patriarch, when he lay down to sleep at Bethel with a stone for his pillow, and the feeling that he was alone. He may be with *you*, also, when you know it not. His name is "Emmanuel, God with us." Not only is he with us in the sense of having been made flesh and dwelt among us, but in the sense of being *in* us still. "Christ *in* you," says St. Paul,— "the hope of glory." He travailed in the pains of spiritual birth till Christ should be *formed in* the Galatian saints to whom he wrote. Jesus himself told his disciples that he would "come" to them, and "make his abode with them." He abides with you, too, although you may not always realize his presence. Mary at the sepulchre did not recognize him as he stood by her, but supposed him to be the gardener. *You* may mistake him, too, as when the disciples saw him walking on the sea; supposed it was a spirit; and cried out for fear. You may be terrified by his presence, even when that presence is in mercy. For he shows himself not always as we may expect or wish. In afflictions and sufferings, he meets us in love, but his aspect seems to us a strange one. When Jacob wept, till he thought his gray hairs must go down under sorrow to the grave, the Lord was leading him in tenderest love, and bringing all things to a happy issue. And will *you* say, "My way is hid from the Lord, and my judgment is passed over from my God?" No; though he may try you sorely, you may be assured that there is mercy behind. The worst storms, such as shake the earth with thunder, and deluge everything with rain, are yet followed by the bow set in the cloud. I am sure you sometimes see that token of the covenant of peace. Take a full view of it, and regard the promise of never-failing mercy of which it is the pledge. Thank God for it, and take courage.

Your affectionate friend,

JAMES MAY.

PHILADELPHIA, December 18, 1862.

MY DEAR FRIEND:

The Saviour's prayer of intercession for you may not embrace, among its objects, the deliverance of yourself, or of his redeemed, from sufferings. Sufferings he may allow as discipline, as fire to purify the gold. But it may embrace the object of your being sanctified through them. I believe that he remembers you with reference to that end. The means to such sanctification may not be what you desire, but God may be trusted for a wise arrangement of them. A parent cannot consent to all a child's wishes, for a child may ignorantly wish for what the parent knows will do him harm. We must consent that God's wisdom prevail over all our devices and desires. He knows better than we what is for our good. You are not permitted to see, beforehand, the way in which he proposes to lead you. You are as a man travelling through the defiles of precipitous mountains, in which the road turns suddenly, every few paces, so that only a very short distance before one can be seen. Still, every step forward brings another space to view. You must proceed thus, step by step. You must be led on your way; as, according to the Lord's Prayer, we are to have our food, not by large supplies, for years beforehand, but *day by day* our *daily* bread. May you have faith so to walk, as by a pace at a time, leaving the future to him who leads the blind by a way that they know not, but always safely, wisely, and in love.

Your affectionate friend,

JAMES MAY.

PHILADELPHIA, January 5, 1863.

MY DEAR FRIEND:

It might seem almost a mockery to give you the greeting of "a happy new year." And yet the Lord may have in store for you, this year, good things beyond all you can allow yourself to hope for. It may be that your place at the marriage supper of the Lamb, and the wedding garment in which you may appear at it, are ready, and only reserved till you shall be called to go in to the marriage.

Trust your whole self in the hands of the glorious Saviour. Trust and live. You need not fear any evil. His rod and staff shall comfort you. You may lean on that staff confidingly. You may be assured of the presence of your God and Saviour. Do not perplex yourself with misgivings as to what is yet to come. "Sufficient unto the day is the evil thereof." When the day of need comes, the grace that is needed will be given. You remember the beautiful illustration of the groundlessness of many of our fears in the Pilgrim's Progress. One of the Pilgrims, who had gone on in advance of Christian, is met running back in fright, because of lions which he had seen in the way. But when Christian walks onward, strong in faith, he finds the lions chained. The lions which so often make afraid, I have no doubt, *you* will find, when you come up to them, to be chained. Take courage, then; and in simplicity of heart, in simple trust in God's covenant care, go onward, without fear. You may be tempted, but the Lord will strengthen you. You may be perplexed, but he will guide you.

Your affectionate friend,

JAMES MAY.

PHILADELPHIA, January 12, 1863.

MY DEAR FRIEND:

You complained, when I saw you to-day, of want of assurance as to your having part in Christ's redemption, and consequently of want of peace.

It does not please God to give us, always, the full shining of his favor. He sometimes draws a cloud over his loving face, and sits in darkness, that we may learn to trust him, even when we cannot see. We must be taught to walk by faith; to go onward in his ways, with full confidence that he will not let a soul that trusteth in him be confounded. He will not contend forever. He will not cast off one that comes to him. Though weeping may endure for a

night, joy cometh in the morning. Lift up your
head, then, for your redemption may be nigh.

Your affectionate friend,

JAMES MAY.

The redemption was nearer than the writer probably supposed.   On the 15th day of January, the sufferer entered into rest. No doubt was entertained, by
those who knew him, of his true piety and thorough
preparation for his end; although, perhaps from a
defective early training, perhaps from the clouding
influence of lengthened pain, he had not such clear
views of his acceptance in Christ Jesus as either
himself or his kind counsellor desired.   There was
humble conscientiousness, sincere desire to do God's
will, entire dependence on his mercy, a recognition
of Christ's work as the only ground for the display of
it, but yet no joyful, continuous sense of personal interest in the great salvation.   Happily, this last is
not required in order to one's peace with God, and
perfect safety through the righteousness and blood
of Jesus.   The light of everlasting love shines round
the soul that truly trusts in Christ, although the
dulled eye of disease and suffering may not perceive
it.   And none who stood around this patient, pious,
trustful sufferer, doubted that, when the weakened
mortal framework fell, his spirit was enabled to rejoice, at once, in the perfect assurance of God's favor.
His end, though not a joyous or triumphant one,
was still, according to the promise, peace.   Excessive suffering impeded expression of his feelings, but
what could be expressed, showed that the eye of faith
looked steadily to Jesus, and that hope was antici-
pating the bright morning of joy after the long night

of weeping. When asked as to his condition, there were broken words and gestures, indicative of quietness of spirit amidst the anguish of great bodily distress. And when questioned further, the hand went to the bosom, the fingers were formed into a cross, and the eyes directed to the heavens, as much as saying that his heart rested upon Christ's atonement, and his trust was that he should be with him in his bliss.

Such cases must be trusted to the mercy of the Saviour, who never casts out any soul that comes to him, and in whom "whosoever believeth" shall not be confounded. Precious in his sight is the death of all his saints. The feeblest is as safe in him as the strongest can be. And heavenly love will present "faultless" in God's presence the weakest spirit that reposes all its trust in Christ.

LETTER TO A FRIEND ON "PRAYER-MEETINGS."

As you refer again, in your last letter, to the question of the canonical propriety of the public prayer-meetings in the Episcopal churches, in Philadelphia, and ask my views, I give you a *resumé* of what I have already written. I put it in the form of questions,

1. Are extemporaneous prayers in public, in *any circumstances*, consistent with adherence to the *principle* of Liturgical provisions for public worship? Bishop Bowman, in his communication to the Committee of the House of Bishops on the Memorial quoted before, says, "I have never considered myself at all bound by the Prayer-Book, when I have found myself in a position for which, evidently, the Prayer-Book has not provided. In all such emergencies, I feel myself as free as a Methodist or a Presbyterian." He expresses, in these words, the minds of a large proportion of our clergy. He has the usage of the Primitive Church and of the Church of England with him. Some, I know, have objected to extemporaneous prayers, even in the family and in the closet. I myself heard the late Bishop Onderdonk say he thought it proper that we should always use a prescribed form of prayer, even in private. But few would go so far as that; at least, in making that *a rule*. Bishop Bowman, you see, differs totally from him; and Bishop White differed almost as much as Bishop Bowman.

2. Are extemporaneous prayers allowable *on occasions for which our Prayer-Book has provided?* Bishop

Bowman says, "Provided the *opening* services are prescribed by authority, I see no unanswerable objection to allowing a freedom in the pulpit, if brethren desire it." "If a clergyman desires it, and his people desire it, I say, let him use his gift" (*i. e.*, of extemporaneous or free prayer). "My greatest objection to it has always been, that it was unauthorized by law." Bishop Bowman here sees no unanswerable objection to the use of extemporaneous prayer, even on occasions of public worship, for which the Prayer-Book *has provided*, if "the *opening* services are prescribed by authority." That is, a clergyman may use extemporaneous prayers, on occasions of public worship, for which the Prayer-Book makes provision, if those prayers *come after* the Prayer-Book service. And that, though there is the objection (the only one, in his view), that they are "unauthorized by law." His language is most just. We may do many things unauthorized by law, provided they be not intrinsically or morally wrong, or not directly forbidden. A clergyman *may* wear a cassock in his daily, unofficial life; a bishop *may* wear an English Episcopal shovel hat, with a rosette (Bishop Doane did so on his return from England), and a short, black apron in front; though, *with us*, these are "unauthorized by law." Each one, in such matters, is to be governed by fashion, taste, or usage. Indeed, our gown, surplice, and white cravat are, among us, unauthorized by law, usage or taste being the only rule; neither rubric nor canon, among us, prescribing anything of the kind, but, simply, that the minister be "decently habited." Extemporaneous prayers *after* the service, as in the Prayer-Book, though unauthorized by law, are not for-

bidden.   Usage for centuries in England, and from
the outset (or certainly from an earlier day than my.
first recollection) among us, sanctions their use *after*
the regular service.   In such case (that is, "if the
opening services are prescribed by authority"), there
is "no unanswerable objection to allowing freedom
(of extemporaneous prayer) in the pulpit."   The gist
of the question, you observe, is the use of extemporaneous prayers, *after* the prescribed use of the Prayer-
Book, on occasions of public worship.   Bishop Bowman, Bishop Burgess (I name these two because
their communications on the subject are now before
me, in print), and hosts of other honest, judicious,
thoughtful persons, agree that extemporaneous
prayers may be used without violating any principle
or positive law, even on occasions of public worship,
provided the *opening* services be according to the
Prayer-Book.   The canon, you remember, prescribes
that "every minister shall, *before* all sermons and
lectures, and on all other occasions of public worship, use the Prayer-Book.   And, *in performing said
service*, no other prayers shall be used," &c.   But it
says nothing as to what may or may not be *after* the
sermon, and *after the said* service.   And here is the
ground on which Bishop Bowman, and the others
referred to, say, and say justly, that they see no unanswerable objection to freedom as to praying, *after*
the *opening* services shall have been performed according to the Prayer-Book.

3. Are the prayer-meetings you refer to "occasions of public worship" such as the canon has in
view?   If so, then the *opening* services ought to be
according to the Prayer-Book (that is, regular morning or evening service); *after* which, "there is no un-

answerable objection to freedom" in praying. If I had been asked this 3d question, without reference to any ground of judgment but my own understanding, I should have promptly answered, Yes, and so decided that the full proper morning or evening service (according to the hour of the day) ought to be used for the *opening* service; *after* which might come in the minister's "own gift." But here I encounter the opinion of the Committee of the House of Bishops, who, in their Report on the Memorial, say : " On occasions or services *other than regular* morning and evening prayer, in established congregations, ministers may, at their discretion, *use such parts* of the Book of Common Prayer, and such lessons, as shall, in their judgment, tend most to edification."

Now, I sum up thus : If the prayer-meetings you refer to put a minister "in a position for which the Prayer-Book has evidently not provided," then, according to Bishop Bowman's view, "he is as free as a Methodist or a Presbyterian."

If those meetings are " occasions of public worship" in the sense of the canon (as I should have said, in my original judgment, they are), then the service prescribed in the Prayer-Book ought to be used as the " *opening* service;" *after* which, as Bishop Bowman says, "there is no unanswerable objection to freedom" in praying.

If, however, though "occasions of public worship," they come under the class of " occasions or services *other than regular morning and evening prayer,*" as meant by the Committee of Bishops (Otey, Doane, A. Potter, Burgess, and Williams), then, in the opinion of those Bishops, the *full* morning or evening service need not be used, but " *parts* of the Book of

Common Prayer" will suffice for an "*opening* service." On neither supposition, are the prayers of our Liturgy to be wholly laid aside. The opinion of the Bishops (just quoted) may leave it an open question, whether those meetings are of the class that require the *whole* service in the Prayer-Book, or of the class "other than regular morning and evening prayer," that require only *parts* of the prayer to be selected by the minister's discretion. In either case, extemporaneous prayers may be allowed afterwards.

A minister is not, in my opinion, liable to a charge of violating ordination vows, who, in those prayer-meetings, sees that the *opening* service is either the full service of the Prayer-Book, or prayers selected from it, so long as the opinion of the Committee of Bishops is regarded as worthy of respect enough to make an open question.

Yours, truly,
JAMES MAY.

LETTER OF GUIDANCE TO A YOUNG CHRISTIAN RELATIVE.

March 20, 1859.

My dear A——:

A very distinguished writer named the book which first gave him reputation, "Saturday Evening." The title, in that case, was figurative and symbolical. If I call this present letter to you Sunday Evening, I shall use the title in the literal sense. I am in my study, alone, on Sunday evening, and, perhaps, may not misuse the hour, if I write you a few lines on a topic, or topics, suited to the holy time. I write not as having " dominion over your faith, but as a helper of your joy." Joy you have, doubtless; the joy which springs from the living fountain of faith in Christ. Perhaps you may be unwilling to speak with assurance as to your joy. You may say you strive to do right, and to find the peace and joy which spring from faith, but that your faith is weak, and your graces generally not as lively as you wish. "Joyfulness through hope" is no mushroom. It does not necessarily spring up in a night, though in some cases, as in that of the Jailer at Philippi, it did so. But that which is to endure through trials, and to last through life, requires, as a general rule, time for being well rooted and strengthened. It springs wholly from faith in Christ. The soul that is vitally joined to Christ by faith has the source and element of joy within, but it may not at first be very manifest. A seed has life in it, but it may require a little time for the growth that will make that life perceptible. I set out with the assumption that you have been joined to the Lord; that you have placed yourself at his feet; that you own him as your Redeemer; and that you have dedicated yourself to him for life. The first stage is simple.

You have been made to see that you are a sinner; a fallen soul; involved in the common ruin of our race; under judgment of death; bound as a slave under sin. In this condition, how can you have life? Not by keeping the commandments, because under those very commandments you are condemned as a sinner. The prisoner in an iron cell, bound in chains, hand and foot, under sentence of death, cannot have life by keeping the law of the land. If he had never committed a crime, then the keeping of that law would have been his life. But now the very same law is his death. "The commandment which was ordained unto life," says St. Paul, "I found to be unto death." Life must come, then, if at all, from another quarter. Grace or mercy must come in. The Gospel proclaims the Saviour the Incarnate Son of God, who comes into our prison, with all sufficiency in himself, and with all power in heaven and earth to forgive sin and discharge from death. The judgment unto death he has received in his own person, borne the curse, and thus taken away sin. Now he calls us to commit ourselves to him; that is, to believe on him; and he, standing for us and in our name, assures full pardon and life. He takes our place under the law, so that, when we are called upon to answer for our sins, *he* is there to answer in our name, and we (if in him, in the new creation) are hid in him, and not to be found. The law takes full satisfaction of him as surety and substitute, and we, in him, are safe. But we must be in him, new creatures in him, having his Spirit, living in him by faith. The early stage of this faith may be one of feebleness. But it is susceptible of growth. St. Paul speaks of those whose " faith grew exceedingly." The growth is, of course, only by the grace of the Spirit of God.

Let me now come to the grand means of growth: I mean the Word of God. The knowledge of the Scriptures, the feeding on their precious truths, and digesting them,—this is to stand first. Without some knowledge of the Word of God, there cannot be even a beginning of faith. " Faith cometh by hearing, and hearing by the Word of God." " Sanctify them through thy truth," our Saviour prays; " thy Word is truth." You do well to attend a Bible-class,—yea, to use any means for treasuring in your mind the Word of God. Much of the Bible may seem to have little application to your case. There are the accounts of the misdoings of many in the Old Testament history; there are the minute details of the Levitical institutions, and the obscure portions of the prophecies. But all are useful; all have their place and their end. You may seem to make but little advancement from day to day. So does a child at school, whose knowledge acquired in any one day may hardly be appreciable. But " oh, the power of littles !" says Dr. Chalmers. It is by littles that we advance. It might be well to pursue a regular course of reading the Bible from the beginning, and, *at the same time*, to study particularly and carefully a particular portion, such as a Gospel, or the Acts, and especially an Epistle. You may find difficulties and obscurities, but they will become plainer as you persevere.

With all your reading the Scriptures, one most important matter must be carefully observed; you must ask the Spirit of God to enlighten you. I believe the truths needful for our salvation are as plainly put down in the text of the Bible as they can be in language, but our understandings need to be opened. All the expositions in the world, no matter how just and authoritative, never can convey the truth properly to the mind, without help from above, for the simple reason that the grand difficulty does not lie in the text of the Bible, as though the meaning were hid for want of clearness and fulness in it, but in the blinded understandings of men. The Spirit of God alone can open the understanding. His grace for this purpose is promised. We should ever pray for it. The good Spirit may lead you, as the blind, by a way you know not. Some things we must be taught by trials. A great Christian said: Two things are needful to make a strong man in Christ,—temptation and prayer. We need not court nor ask for trials. They will come soon enough, and be hard enough to bear when they come. May the gracious Spirit ever teach and guide you.

Your affectionate uncle,
JAMES MAY.

LETTER TO A MINISTER

IN AN IMPORTANT BUT SOMEWHAT TRYING SPHERE.

THEOLOGICAL SEMINARY, March 24, 1851.

MY DEAR BROTHER:

In my garden is a tree of great promise; an apple-tree; a sapling full of wholesome juices, vigorous in growth, and fruit-bearing. Looking on it one day, with much complacency and bright hope, I thought I saw dangers from the violence of tempests. Indeed, I had seen it seized by furious winds, which made its branches whisk about as if sweeping the air; its trunk was violently writhed, and I began to fear lest it might be wrenched from its roots and borne away. To make it as sure as I could, I looked about for a support, and found a hard, dry, and very unsightly stake. This I carefully set against it. Though the stake was in itself valueless, yet it aided the tree, which now stands erect, awaiting the return of the genial sun to bring out its blossoms and ripen its fruit. My heart is gladdened. This account is properly historical, and when you come again to Maywood, you may behold the tree's *objective being*. But I recite the story for an allegory. The garden is ——; the youthful tree, rich in juices, and fruit-bearing, is my brother ——; the tempests are the worldliness, and flatteries, and gainsayings of the people; the unsightly stake, dry and hard, and of no inherent value, yet, in proper posture, fitted to give some aid and support, is the present writer. Now, my brother, let me speak freely, out of my heart's fulness. My heart is full; was made so, when I heard you (while

here) speak of your position in ——, your trials, &c.,
&c. I was ready to glorify God on your behalf.
By grace we are saved. By the grace of God we
are what we are. As my heart went with your
heart, I thought of my tree and of the fury of tempests. Then I bethought myself of being a stake,
to set up against you. The roughness and hardness
thereof, it seemed to me, would not be considered,
provided it served to give aid and support. Without assuming, in regard to my apple-tree, any peculiar liability to be borne away, I knew it to be in the
nature of all trees, that they might be endangered
by storms. My brother in —— has stood well; God
has magnified his grace in sustaining him. Still, as
he is flesh, and as —— is, perhaps, quite as much
Satan's seat as was Pergamos, a brother's sympathy
may not be useless. My brother, I give way to my
sympathy for you; you have run well; you do run
well. Let not the Devil hinder you, whether he come
in the shape of sedulous friendship, taking you by
the arm, whispering soft flattery in your ears, and
proposing to set you on the pinnacle of the temple,
where you can have the gaze of a crowd while you
make a flight; or in the shape of denunciation, and
reproach, and calumny, as when he would charge
you with Puritanism, and cant, and narrowness of
mind, and propagate lies concerning you. Two
sources of danger are open to you; one, that of direct opposition and threats. Satan may hint a loss
of popularity, if you be too faithful, and will not
give way a little to the prejudices and deeply rooted
customs and habits of worldly men. Or he may try
to get into your heart by the door of vanity, by
means of his flattering tongue. He may tell you of

the patronage of great men, whom a little easiness of doctrine and of discipline may bring over by degrees. He may show you your success, and insinuate that *you* have builded this great Babylon; and so may strive to puff you up, and make you unsteady of purpose, or unwatchful, while he prepares for an effective attempt at your overthrow. You are not ignorant of his devices. My object in writing is not to instruct you, for I have need to be taught of you, but to express sympathy and brotherly fellowship. I cannot infuse into you life or spirit, or even give you light. My stake does nothing of the kind to my tree; the rich and living juices come from another source, the genial influences of the heavens. Yet the stake may not be useless. Now, brother, you, who have fought a good warfare, and occupy an important fortress, be strong in the Lord. Keep your position clear of all embarrassments. As you have begun, so continue. Let the world see, and let Satan see, and God will see, that you mean, by divine grace, to be faithful. Remember, the true weapon, whether for attack or defence, is the sword of the Spirit, the Word of God,—the pure, simple Word of God. Preach and teach out of the Bible, in the spirit of the Bible. The pure Gospel, to superstitious, carnal Jews, a stumbling-block; and to proud, rationalistic Greeks (the infidel or rationalizing man in high stations), foolishness, is the power of God to all who believe. Let not the Cross be without effect through too much wisdom of words. Be thou an example to the flock, in these days of worldly wisdom, and worldly occupations, and amusements; of shallow religion, and of deep superstition, and cold formality, in which Puseyism, and Popery, and a diluted Gospel are welcomed in so many quarters; let it be seen that you mean to stand as you have done; and while speaking in love, let it be the speaking of the truth. Be Elijah before Ahab; be John Baptist before Herod; be Paul before Agrippa; be Luther at Worms; be Huss at Constance; be Ridley at the stake. Give yourself wholly to the things to which now God calls you. Make full proof of your ministry. Your brethren look on, and a great crowd of witnesses look on; your own conscience, and God, our Saviour and Lord, look on. Let the vain, thoughtless, self-willed lovers of pleasure about you,—the veterans in Satan's service, as well as the raw recruits,—know distinctly what God says, and how he will judge. Let the truth and justice of God speak in thunder from Sinai, and shake the whole camp of idolatrous Israel. Then preach Christ crucified; lift him up above all men and all men's pride, and let him be seen, not merely the symbol, but the actual living source, of life, and peace, and hope, to men dying in sin and misery. Tell the seekers of pleasure, who would have the world's favors, and at the same time assume the name of followers of Christ, that their Judge eternal cannot be mocked. He sees through all their vain words and empty forms of confessing his name. He will have none of it. "Ye cannot serve God and mammon," says he. To the souls of hollow, empty professors of his name, he will say, "I never knew you; depart from me, ye workers of iniquity." Those poor, self-deceived souls, who think they can enjoy the pleasure of sin during the week, and drink the Lord's cup on Sunday; who can dance to Satan's music one day, and with solemn gesture stand to chant the Lord's songs the next day,—tell them what the truth is. They have their pains for nothing. It is useless to trouble themselves with the burden of worshipping the Lord, or waiting in his courts. He will have no such sacrifices as they offer. Their incense is an abomination. Call on Christians, also, to be faithful; separate from the world; to let their light shine, to bear a clear and distinct testimony for truth and godliness.

In all, do not fear; God can make you stand in all storms. Be but faithful in his word. Hold fast the pure Gospel, and preach nothing but Christ and him crucified. If sometimes you fall into trials for so doing, remember it is said, "Blessed is the man that endureth temptation." Hottest fires are best for purifying gold. Now, while you have a brother's sympathies and prayers, I trust you may ever have what is of infinitely higher worth,—wisdom, and strength, and life, from our Great Head.

You may think, perhaps, I am writing without a call to do so; that I am making an occasion which does not properly exist for such an epistle. A brother's kindness and sympathy have sought an utterance. If the utterance be out of place, or not called for, I submit. I am not judge; I only know my own feelings, and in the matter am led by them. I pretend to be nothing more than an old, unsightly stake, set up as a prop for a young, vigorous, fruitful tree. At all events,

Your affectionate brother,
JAMES MAY.

LETTER RESPECTING ATTENDANCE AT CONVENTION.

A LETTER written in the unreserved and open confidence of private friendship must usually be sacred. But this which follows contains so clear a portrait of himself, from Dr. May's own hand, that a memoir of him would hardly be complete without it. It came to hand from Virginia, after all else was in the press.

THEOLOGICAL SEMINARY, May 14, 1854.

MY DEAR BROTHER:

I am much obliged to you for your kind letter from New York, and for your very *non*-"presumptuous advice" about going to Convention. I have a very high opinion of Mrs. May's "rightness of mind," a much higher one than any one else, and for a better reason; and that is, because I know her better than any one else. But it is the nature of advice to be advisory, not judicial nor mandatory. And so both she and I regard it. In itself, the thing recommended is good, very good, most excellent. But, *in generalibus latet dolus.* We cannot govern ourselves, nor the world, by the literality of general rules. For instance, the general rule forbids any manner of work on the Sabbath day; and yet we should err if thereby we shut ourselves out from works of charity. The rule of going to Convention is most excellent, but particular persons on particular occasions may be excepted. The general rule that you should visit us every time you get as near as Alexandria, and a good deal oftener, is good; and yet I do not know but that, by some means (as by a "*non-natural*" sense put on the rule), you excuse yourself. I hope I have demonstrated that there may be cases in which one may be excused for not going to Convention. Now, let me show that such a case is mine. I must here make a preliminary remark. You do not know me, if you suppose that I do not enjoy meeting with brethren in the ministry. I know of no greater joy on earth. It refreshes, cheers, and strengthens me. It is the communion of saints; it is a heavenly feast; it enkindles holy fire; it melts, heats, and promotes true unity by the fusion of all into one; it lifts hands that hang down, and strengthens feeble knees; it is music in the soul, such as may lift the emotions in rapture; it is heaven begun on earth. This I know from most precious experience. It moves my soul to think of it. I know I should rejoice in the company of brethren in a Virginia Convention. God forbid that I should, by any rule, be shut out from such a privilege. I hope to see a day when I may again enjoy it.

As I know of no special good I could do in going to Convention this year, I had never allowed myself to think of going, because of the distance, though this is greatly reduced by railroad; yet this I did not anticipate when I allowed my mind to settle down in the persuasion that it is best for me to remain at home. Some men are praised for being *good listeners* while others speak.   Is there no praise in being a good stayer-at-home?   Some must talk and some must go from home, for business, office, and high duty require it.   I do not fall within that category.   My office and duty are here, unless some call of Providence withdraws me.   I trust I am ready to obey such call.   The time was when I was ambitious.   While a youth I had high aspirations and schemes, and was agitated by restless desires for the great things of this world.   I think I may say that spirit in me is broken.   The Lord has led me by a way that I knew not.   I have been put under a yoke. Oh! how much I struggled; yea, I may say, fought and rebelled.   I was as a bullock unaccustomed to the yoke.   Nature, poor fallen nature, was proud, and vain, and stout, and selfish.   It seemed as if submission was out of the question.   Convictions of truth and duty, though clear and unquestionable, seemed not of force to check an untamed spirit. *Many, many* times has the contest cost me tears in my chamber, and even in the public streets.   I was a great sinner, a wicked rebel.   Years did not see the end of this conflict; nay, even twenty, or five and twenty, did not count its time.   But I trust it is over.   Whether it be by the mastery of grace, or by the mere exhaustion of nature, the proud heart is broken.   I have seen enough of this world.   I shrink into quietness.   The Gospel is sweet to my wounded soul.   It is a most precious balm.   It is heavenly. The truth that the Son of God, (not a creature, but) the eternal Son of God, is the Saviour of poor lost sinners such as I; that he died under the burden of our sins, and now lives in Divine power to give repentance and forgiveness, is the most glorious, the most precious, the most quickening truth ever proclaimed in the hearing of men from the foundation of the world. I have some hope for myself in that blessed truth. When it comes to my spirit, oh! it is like living waters to a soul dying of thirst. To preach this to others is to me, at times, unspeakably joyful. My soul rises with the theme. It is refreshed in the act of giving these living waters to others who are thirsty.

Perhaps I err in pouring out to you thus my private emotions. You may be led to presume that I have had more experience in the good things of the Gospel than I have had. I have been a dull, heavy, reluctant, impatient learner. The point to which I bring all I have said is, that I shrink from public places. Whether it be weakness, or want of courage and of energy, I do not know; but I confess to being a conquered man. I yield and sink down. Many schemes and hopes which, in my little sphere, seemed big, are wholly gone, like dreams. I long for quietness, and in quietness (if the Lord so favor me) to preach Christ and Him crucified. Some of my friends say I preach Christ too exclusively; that I lack variety, and do not dwell on other seasonable or interesting topics. But I excuse myself. Others do that thing (I mean touch on other topics), and in more life than I can. My mission (if I have any) is in quietness to preach Christ.

Now you may understand that if I stay at home, it is from no want of interest in my brethren. Truly, they are dear to me; dear for Christ's sake. But not having now any call (so far as I see) to leave home, may I not quietly attend to what concerns me here? As to the good to be done to the Seminary and the Review* by my being at Convention, I have no perception. According to your own showing, too, it is no great matter. If I pray for you all, may I not do something? God forbid that I should cease to pray for you. Some men are born to be legislators (as we say, *poeta nascitur, non fit*). I was not. I shall try to conserve the laws when made (reserving the right of opinion about them, however). I do not think I am a croaker. I believe the world is about as good as it used to be, and I cannot but hope for the happy progress of pure religion. But oh! that we could pray and look for the " pouring out of the Spirit from on high." We may not be looking as we ought for his coming upon us. We grieve him by our pride and self-righteousness. We may make canons till we fill volumes, such as the *Corpus Juris canonici* and the *Corpus Juris civilis* put together. We may fill the land with seminaries, and multiply bishops like States, and build Gothic churches, and practice all the little rules of ecclesiology; but what will all come to, if the Spirit of God be withheld? We shall have the clay figure, without the breath of life. I am ashamed, for myself, when I think how little the Spirit is sought for. My dear brother, you know how vain are all attemps to promote life and unity in the Church, without the living power of the Holy Ghost. I fear we begin at the wrong side, that is the outside, for true godliness is the Spirit dwelling

---

* The " Protestant Episcopal Review," which, during a large part of its existence, was under the editorship of Dr. May.

inwardly, as a well of living waters. What are all attempts at unity, without his indwelling? They are iron bands around gnarled trunks, keeping together an unsightly and useless mass, without life or growth. I am ashamed of my letter; and now, as I finish it, have great scruples about sending it. It is so full of myself that I fear you will think me incapable of anything but egotism. Excuse me, and take a pledge of love for yourself and all the brethren from your brother,

JAMES MAY.

www.ingramcontent.com/pod-product-compliance
Lightning Source LLC
Chambersburg PA
CBHW022351020726
47500CB00002B/230